"Where am I to asked.

"There's a guest bedroom across the hall." Cristiano pushed open the door opposite his own. She turned to glance at him and that was her mistake. Her breath came out in a rush as heat flared between them. He put his hand on her wrist.

"Don't, Cristiano," she whispered.

"Don't what?"

"Don't touch me."

"Don't tempt you?" He stroked the silky skin of her inner wrist with his thumb. "Is that what you mean?" Laurel remained frozen, her pulse hammering. "Why deny what is between us, *bella*?"

"There's nothing between us." She had to nearly gasp the words out.

"Your body begs to differ." Cristiano could see the indecision in her fractured gaze, the desire as well as the doubt. "Stop worrying so much. What are you afraid of?" he murmured, his lips very nearly brushing hers.

"This," she whispered, and then Cristiano kissed her.

After spending three years as a die-hard New Yorker, **Kate Hewitt** now lives in a small village in the English Lake District with her husband, their five children and a golden retriever. In addition to writing intensely emotional stories, she loves reading, baking and playing chess with her son—she has yet to win against him, but she continues to try. Learn more about Kate at kate-hewitt.com.

Books by Kate Hewitt

Harlequin Presents

Moretti's Marriage Command
Inherited by Ferranti

One Night With Consequences

Engaged for Her Enemy's Heir
Larenzo's Christmas Baby

Seduced by a Sheikh

The Secret Heir of Alazar
The Forced Bride of Alazar

The Billionaire's Legacy

A Di Sione for the Greek's Pleasure

Secret Heirs of Billionaires

Demetriou Demands His Child

The Marakaios Brides

The Marakaios Marriage
The Marakaios Baby

Visit the Author Profile page at Harlequin.com for more titles.

Kate Hewitt

THE INNOCENT'S ONE-NIGHT SURRENDER

HARLEQUIN PRESENTS®

Recycling programs
for this product may
not exist in your area.

ISBN-13: 978-1-335-41903-3

The Innocent's One-Night Surrender

First North American publication 2017

Copyright © 2017 by Kate Hewitt

Printed in U.S.A.

HARLEQUIN®
TM www.Harlequin.com

THE INNOCENT'S
ONE-NIGHT SURRENDER

To Jenna. Thanks for spurring me on with this book! Love being able to chat with you. Love, K.

CHAPTER ONE

LAUREL FORRESTER BURST from the hotel room like a
bullet from a gun, aiming for the lift down the hall.
Her breath came in tearing gasps and she stumbled
in the heels she wasn't used to wearing—stupid, sky-
high stilettos her mother had insisted on.

She heard the sound of the door to the executive
suite being wrenched open behind her and then heavy
footfalls.

'Come back here, you stupid little—'

With a mewling gasp of terror, Laurel put on a
burst of speed, racing around the corner. The gleaming black doors of the lift shimmered ahead of her, a
promise of freedom.

'Wait until I...'

She closed her mind to Rico Bavasso's threats and
stabbed the button for the lift with a shaking finger.
Please, please open. Save me...

Bavasso came round the corner, moving swiftly for
a man pushing sixty. Laurel risked a glance back and
then wished she hadn't. Three diagonal cuts slashed
one of his lean cheeks, where she'd scratched him,
blood oozing down his face in crimson, pearly droplets.

Please, please open. If the lift doors didn't open,

she didn't know what she'd do. Fight for her safety, for her life. Go down kicking and screaming, because go down she would. Bavasso might be older but he was big, strong and angry, and she was five-foot-four and just a little over a hundred pounds soaking wet.

With a glorious ping the doors opened and Laurel threw herself inside, bruising her shoulder against the far wall before she scrambled upright. She pushed just about every button she could, anything to get her away from the hell that had erupted with Bavasso's demands and grabs, his insistence that he would get what he'd paid for. What her mother had promised him.

Bile rose in Laurel's throat at that memory and she choked it down. She didn't have the luxury of memories or even thoughts in this moment. This was about basic survival. She pushed the 'door close' button repeatedly as Bavasso stumbled towards the lift, a smile of triumph curving his cold mouth, his glowering face thrust forward. His bow tie was askew, his tuxedo shirt straining against the buttons as he reached one hand forward to keep the doors from closing. Laurel shrank back against the lift wall, her heart beating in her chest like some wild, winged thing.

'I've got you, you little slut.'

Laurel kicked off one of her wretched stilettos and swung it at Bavasso's grasping hand. He let out a howl of outrage and yanked it back, his palm impaled by the dagger-sharp heel. The doors closed and then the lift was soaring upwards and Laurel was safe, *safe*.

She let out a sob of both terror and relief, her senses overwhelmed by what had happened—and what had almost happened, but thankfully hadn't. Her trembling legs felt weak and watery and she sank onto the floor, drawing her knees up to her chest as shudders wracked her body. *That had been so close.*

But she wasn't out of danger yet. She still had to get out of this hotel, out of Rome. Bavasso had her handbag in his hotel room, as well as his security detail waiting down in the foyer. Laurel had seen them when he'd been playing baccarat, standing around like stony-faced gorillas, eyes darting around the casino floor, looking for threats. And now she was one.

What would he do? Over the last two days' acquaintance he'd been sleek and charming, although admittedly paying her more attention than she'd have liked, considering he was her mother's latest love interest. He also seemed arrogant and entitled, and she feared he might not let this lie. And what about her mother? Was Elizabeth safe? Would Bavasso turn on her—or had she really been part of it all along, as he'd implied? *I'm only taking what your mother promised me.*

Surely not? Surely her mother wouldn't have sold her off like a cow at auction? With another cry Laurel covered her face, the tumult of the evening too much to bear. She should never have agreed to come to Rome, to play a part so she could get what she wanted. And yet she had. She'd weighed it up in her mind and she'd decided it was worth it. One last favour and then she'd finally be free. Except she wasn't free now. She didn't feel remotely free.

The doors opened and Laurel lifted her head, shrinking back, half-expecting Bavasso to be there, waiting. But, no; the lift opened directly into what looked like a private suite, twice as elegant and spacious as the one Laurel had just fled.

She scrambled to her feet, pulling on the hem of the

short sparkly dress of silver satin that had also been her mother's choice. *Bavasso wants to see a lovely young woman in her prime, not some dowdy wallflower. He's a discriminating man, Laurel.* Now she was afraid she understood all that had meant.

Laurel knew she couldn't stay in the lift; the doors would close and then the lift would start heading down again, back to Bavasso or his goons, somewhere she definitely didn't want to be. Cautiously Laurel took a step out, onto a floor of polished black marble. Floor-to-ceiling windows were visible in every direction, giving a panoramic view of the Eternal City, lights shimmering in the darkness.

Modern-looking sofas of black leather and gleaming chrome were scattered around, the soaring space lit only by a few minimalistic table lamps, so it took Laurel a stunned second to realise there was someone in the room with her.

A man stood at its centre dressed in black trousers and a charcoal-grey shirt that was open at the throat. His hair was black and cropped close to his head, his eyes a piercing grey, the same colour as his shirt. His arms were folded, emphasising impressive biceps, and everything about him radiated power. Control. *Danger.*

Laurel's breath hitched and she froze where she stood, dawning realisation, relief and fear colliding inside her with an almighty crash. *Could it be...?*

Then he spoke, a voice like molten silver, pitched low. His tone was both authoritative and sensual, winding around her shattered senses, pulling them tight.

'Hello, Laurel.'

She gave a little gasp of surprise even though she'd known, deep inside, that it was him. That it had to be him. The awareness she felt of him didn't make sense, considering they were near strangers, yet she wasn't surprised by it at all.

'Cristiano.' She let out a little laugh of relief; the adrenalin still coursing through her body made her feel shaky and weak. Or maybe he was making her feel shaky and weak, standing there like a rock-solid pillar, arms still folded, face expressionless in the dim light. 'Thank God.'

He arched one dark slash of an eyebrow, his gaze travelling to her tiny, torn dress. 'Things get a little out of hand?'

Laurel glanced down at her dress, an embarrassed flush sweeping over her along with all the other overwhelming emotions. The dress was practically indecent, a spangled slip that revealed far too much thigh and cleavage. One of the straps had torn from the bodice, so the dress gaped even more. She wasn't even wearing a bra, only a tiny scrap of a thong. And, from the hard look in her stepbrother's eyes, Laurel suspected he knew it—and wasn't impressed.

She took a deep breath, trying to gather her scattered wits. Her head was spinning from everything that had happened, and her legs still felt weak. She longed to sit down, to *breathe*, to figure out how she'd got here and what on earth she was going to do next. 'I didn't even know you were here.'

'Didn't you?'

'No, of course not…' Laurel frowned, belatedly registering Cristiano's cool tone, the look of mocking censure in his iron gaze. And then she remembered the last time she'd seen him, ten years ago, when she'd been a silly fourteen-year-old to his manly twenty-three, and when she'd practically thrown herself at him as part of a stupid teenaged dare.

'I don't even know where I am,' she said, trying to smile, but her lips didn't seem to be working properly. They just wobbled.

'You're in the penthouse suite of La Sirena. My private home.'

'Oh.' So she'd pushed *that* button? But how had she been granted access? 'Well, I'm glad the doors opened up here. Very glad.'

'I'm sure you are.' There was a note of sardonic amusement in his voice that Laurel felt too scatter-brained to understand at the moment. It sounded as if he was referencing something she was meant to know about and didn't. Unless he was referring to her stupid schoolgirl crush all those years ago. Laurel doubted that. She doubted her one clumsy attempt at a kiss—he'd pushed her firmly away before she'd so much as made contact—had stayed in Cristiano's memory for more than a millisecond. He'd been that unimpressed.

'Do you mind if I clean myself up?' she asked. 'I feel...' Dirty. She felt dirty. But Cristiano didn't need to know that. He was already looking at her as if he thought she was, a realisation that made heat scorch Laurel's face once more. She knew she was wearing a slinky, slutty get-up, but did he have any right to judge her? Although, considering her actions tonight, perhaps he did.

'Be my guest.' Cristiano gestured towards a corridor that led to the suite's bedrooms. 'You'll find everything you need in one of the bathrooms.'

'Thank you,' Laurel answered, her tone turning a bit haughty to cover her confusion—and her guilt. If she could have picked the circumstances in which she ever saw her stepbrother again, these would not have been them. Not by a million awful miles.

Was it just the way she was dressed or was there another reason he was being so cold? Not that they'd ever had much of a relationship, or one at all. Her mother had been married to his father for three years, but in that time Laurel had only met Cristiano twice. Once after the wedding, when he'd had a blazing argument with his father, Lorenzo Ferrero, and then stormed out. And the second time when he'd come home for some reason and she'd attempted, in pathetic, girlish naivety, to impress him.

Six months later Lorenzo had divorced Elizabeth and Laurel and her mother had high-tailed it back to Illinois, with nothing but a pocketful of jewellery to fund Elizabeth's often exorbitant lifestyle. Ferrero had had a water-tight pre-nup, and her mother did like to spend money…

Cristiano was still staring at her, arms folded, the emotion in his silver eyes fathomless. What had she expected him to say? Do? He'd never expressed any familial concern or even interest in her before.

She was a stranger to him, or near enough to it, just as he was to her—or should be, except for the fact that out of idle curiosity—or perhaps, shamefully, something a little deeper than that—she'd followed his exploits on social media and scanned the many tabloid articles about his playboy lifestyle. She'd always been fascinated by this man who had loomed on the periphery of her life, dark and powerful, when she'd been an innocent teenaged girl emerging shyly from her chrysalis of gawkiness into uncertain womanhood.

It truly stunned her that she was in his penthouse now, although she supposed, if she stopped long enough to think rationally about it, she shouldn't have been that surprised. She'd known the hotel where they'd met Bavasso was owned by Cristiano. She just hadn't expected actually to see him.

Cristiano's mouth curved in a smile that held neither humour nor warmth. His eyes glittered like burnished mirrors, reflecting nothing. 'You said you wanted to clean yourself up?' he prompted.

'Yes.' Laurel realised she was staring but it was hard not to stare at a man who was so starkly beautiful, so arrogantly attractive. The silk of his shirt clung to his well-defined pectoral muscles and the narrow trousers emphasised lean hips and powerful thighs. But beyond the impressive musculature of his body was the aura he possessed, the lethal authority and latent sexuality he emanated from every perfect pore—and that was what made Laurel stare. And not just stare, but *imagine*, shadowy, vague thoughts and images that danced through her mind, awakening longings that been dormant for her whole life. Thankfully they remained shadowy, falling back and leaving a streak of restless heat in their wake.

Staring at him now, taking in the arrogant tilt of his head, the dark, winged eyebrows, the sculpted mouth formed into a hard, hard line—he looked just the same as he had ten years ago. Perhaps he was a bit more muscular now, a bit more powerful. He'd made his own millions in the last decade, she knew, in property, casinos and hotels, at the highest end of the market.

He'd also, according to the tabloids, had dozens and dozens of mistresses—Hollywood actresses and European supermodels who graced his arm like the most expensive accessories, and, if the papers were to be believed—and Laurel suspected they were—were discarded after a matter of days.

It seemed incredible to her that she'd actually tried, in a clumsy, desperate way, to make him like her gawky teenaged self. The realisation made her cringe even now—especially now—yet surely Cristiano didn't remember that? He'd swatted her away like a fly.

Just the memory made flustered confusion sweep through her and quickly she turned away, afraid that Cristiano would see her uncertainty. He'd seen too much already, starting with this skimpy dress.

'Thank you,' she mumbled again and then, not wanting to prolong her agony, she hurried down the hall.

Cristiano watched Laurel scurry down the hall like a frightened rabbit. A sexy frightened rabbit, wearing far too little clothing for his comfort, and only one shoe. He turned away, his jaw tightening, the flare of sexual attraction arrowing through him annoying him further. He hadn't expected to feel it quite so strongly, especially now that he knew what she was like.

When he'd seen Laurel Forrester swan into La Sirena this evening, dressed like a hooker and on the arm of a man who made his skin crawl, he'd felt shock slice through him. It was ten years since he'd last seen her; she looked a whole lot more grown up now, yet he'd recognised her. Instantly.

That second of stunned amazement had morphed into a deep, sick disappointment that settled in his gut, a leaden weight that was absurd, because if he'd had to think about it for a second he'd have known Laurel would be just like her mother—a craven, amoral gold-digger playing for her best chance. She'd shown her true colours at just fourteen years old, after all, and heaven knew the apple didn't usually fall far from the tree.

Which was why he had been so determined to cut off all his ties with his own father. The last thing he wanted to do was make the mistakes Lorenzo Ferrero had, chasing after some ridiculous and ever-elusive happily-ever-after and becoming increasingly more desperate to find it. Letting himself be used, hurt and humiliated, and for what? An amorphous emotion that didn't really exist, or at least shouldn't. Love.

Cristiano strolled towards the window, shoving his hands deep into his trouser pockets as he mused on what lay in store for Laurel…and for him. He'd watched her on the casino floor, draped on Bavasso's arm, her attempts at flirting cringingly over the top and obvious. She might be many things but what she definitely wasn't was a good actress.

Bavasso, of course, had lapped it up and demanded more. A lot more, apparently, because after Cristiano had left the floor he'd stayed by the bank of security cameras in his flat, watching her, waiting—but for what? He was acting obsessed, which was stupid, but he hadn't been able to keep himself from doing it.

He'd told himself it was because of their past—because he knew her mother was a thief and he had no intention of letting her fleece any of his customers, even one as unpleasant as Rico Bavasso. He'd told himself that, but he didn't completely buy it.

Then everything in him had frozen and clenched hard when he'd seen her leave the casino floor, Bavasso holding her hand, practically dragging her towards the lifts. But she'd gone. She'd been *smiling*. For some reason that smile had reached a vulnerable place he hated the thought of even possessing.

Cristiano didn't know what had happened upstairs in the hotel suite but he could guess all too easily. Still he'd stayed by the cameras, which was why he'd seen her running for the lifts, as if the hounds of hell were chasing her—or just one lascivious one. Whatever game she was playing, she'd decided not to see it to the finish. And, while Cristiano certainly believed in a woman's right to say no whenever she chose to, it didn't change his opinion of Laurel Forrester one iota.

On the cameras he'd watched her hit all the buttons, including the one for the penthouse. The lift doors to the penthouse were always locked, but with one flip of a switch Cristiano had sent Laurel straight up to him.

And now here she was.

The only question that remained was, what was he going to do with her?

He narrowed his gaze as he looked out of the window, the Colosseum lit up at night, a beacon to the city. He'd brought Laurel up here because she'd needed rescuing and he was a man of honour.

But honour only extended so far. And now, with the lift doors locked again, the only person Laurel needed rescuing from was him.

CHAPTER TWO

LAUREL PEEKED INTO the first room on the left, a sumptuous bedroom with an *en suite* bathroom, and then she tiptoed over thick, white pile carpet, past a huge king-sized bed on its own dais with a rumpled black satin duvet. This was where Cristiano slept, and she sensed him in every sleek and powerful line of the room. She smelled him too—that spicy aftershave and something else, something infinitely more male that wound through her senses and ignited fireworks in her belly. Fireworks she was going to do her best to ignore.

Her curious gaze took in the room's stark elements—bed, bureau, view. No personal objects or mementoes, no photographs or knick-knacks. Not even a book. No sign of a woman, either, so perhaps he was between mistresses. But why was she looking? Laurel bolted for the bathroom, locking the door behind her.

The bathroom was just as elegantly stark as the bedroom, and almost as big. An enormous sunken black marble tub with gold taps, a separate infinity shower bigger than her bedroom back home and double sinks. Laurel registered the heat coming through the quarry tiles beneath her feet and let out a shuddery sigh, the events of the last few hours slamming into her all over her again.

The endless evening at the casino, while Rico had played baccarat and given her lascivious looks that Laurel had told herself were in her imagination. They had to be. Bavasso liked her mother. Her mother had said she was hoping for a ring, for goodness' sake. He wouldn't look at her. The only reason she was meeting him was to give her mother her blessing.

Wasn't it?

Then the moment when he'd asked her to go upstairs, and Laurel had given her mother a frantic look. Elizabeth had smiled and had told her she'd be along in a few minutes and they'd all have champagne to celebrate. And Laurel had believed her. Of course she had believed her. Elizabeth was her mother and, while she'd done some questionable things over the years, she'd never done anything like this.

Laurel closed her eyes as she tried to will back the pain of the betrayal. Although, betrayal wasn't the right word, not really, because Elizabeth hadn't promised anything but the cold, hard cash she knew Laurel needed… And Laurel had been willing to take it. Did that make her any better than her mother, a woman who was always on the prowl for a man to fund her lifestyle?

Taking a deep breath, Laurel opened her eyes and then shrugged off the satin slip of a dress. It pooled at her feet and, overcome suddenly with a remorse so strong it felt like a physical illness, cramping her stomach and making her gorge rise, she kicked the offending garment into the corner of the room.

But that wasn't enough—Laurel could still see the

dress, a rumpled pile of silver, and with a little cry she snatched it up and pulled. The thin fabric tore easily, and within seconds the dress was in bright, glittering ribbons that she stuffed into the bin. Then she realised it was remarkably unwise to destroy the one piece of clothing she had. Was she meant to go confront Cristiano in nothing but a lacy thong? *That* would go over well.

With a groan, Laurel turned on the shower. She needed to wash and scrub off the scent of the expensive, cloying cologne that Rico Bavasso wore before she thought about what could she do—or what could she wear.

She stepped under the powerful jets, letting the water stream over and wash away her regrets…if only it could. She never should have agreed to her mother's plan. Never should have sold her soul for a flimsy promise her mother now might not even keep. And if she didn't…

Laurel's heart lurched. It didn't feel fair that she wanted so little, worked so hard and might still end up with nothing. But she knew there was no point in whining or crying about it. She'd made her own choices, and they hadn't all been good ones. Some of them had been extraordinarily bad. Somehow she had to rescue what she could from the rubble of the last few hours.

She stayed in the bathroom for as long as she could, first under the soothing spray of the shower, and then brushing her hair. Thankfully there was a thick navy terrycloth robe hanging on the door and she swathed herself in it, grateful that it covered her from her neck to her toes. She needed the armour, flimsy as it was.

She also needed time to figure out a plan—and how to present it to Cristiano. She had, unfortunately, extremely limited resources or options. She'd left her handbag behind in Bavasso's hotel room, with her money, driving licence and hotel key. Her passport, at least, was in the safe back at the shabby *pensione* where she and her mother were staying. But how was she going to get there? What if Bavasso was waiting for her?

Taking a deep breath, she decided it was time to face the music. Face Cristiano…a prospect that made her insides lurch with alarm even as a little ripple of anticipation shivered through her. She was looking forward to seeing him, even sparring with him, although heaven knew she shouldn't be.

The relief she'd felt at being rescued, however accidentally, from Rico Bavasso's clutches had dissolved, replaced with an uncomfortable realisation that there was no love lost between Cristiano and her, or Cristiano's father and her mother. A bitter divorce had put paid to any family reunions, and if he remembered Laurel's schoolgirl crush he certainly didn't do so fondly. But surely he'd help her, a woman so obviously in distress and need? Cool and remote he might be, but he was—she hoped—a man of honour.

With nothing left to lose, Laurel headed back out to the suite's sitting room. Cristiano was stretched out on one of the sofas, his long, muscular legs propped on a glass-and-chrome coffee table, his high-tech smart phone in one hand as he scrolled through messages. He slid it into his pocket and stood up, all graceful, fluid urbanity, as she came into the room.

'Feel better?' he asked with a sardonic lift of one eyebrow.

'Yes, thank you. Your shower is amazing.' Her voice sounded thin and wavering, the voice of a girl rather than a woman. Laurel straightened. Cristiano might reduce her insides to quivering jelly—it was hard not to be affected and, yes, dazzled, by a man who exuded so much potent, masculine sexuality—but she could still take control of this conversation. 'I need to ask a favour of you.'

Cristiano looked unsurprised. 'Oh?' His voice was mild and enquiring, yet something dark pulsed underneath that innocuous tone, something that made Laurel feel even warier than she already did.

'Could you please send someone—one of your staff, perhaps—to my hotel? I need my things—my clothes and my passport.' She lifted her chin, forcing herself to meet his sardonic, silvery gaze. 'I'm intending to leave Rome as soon as possible.'

He cocked his head. 'Things not work out to your satisfaction here, then?'

She couldn't miss the mocking note in his voice and a flush swept over her. Still she kept his gaze. 'No.'

'Rico Bavasso doesn't like to be thwarted, you know,' Cristiano said after a moment when he continued simply to study her, an inspection so thorough Laurel felt as if he could see beneath the big, bulky robe she wore.

'I guessed as much, which is why I'm planning on leaving the country.'

'You think it will be that easy?'

Unease tightened in her gut and flared through her insides. 'What do you mean?'

'Bavasso is a powerful and unpleasant man,' Cristiano stated flatly. 'You chose the wrong mark, *bella*.'

She stared at him, that one work reverberating through her. *Mark*. So he thought she was a con artist, one step up from a prostitute, perhaps. She shouldn't care. She shouldn't even be surprised. She'd been acting like one, more or less, all evening, even if she'd never meant things to unravel the way they had. Shame burned deep, singeing her conscience, her soul. Why had she been so stupid; so desperate?

And as for Bavasso being both powerful and unpleasant…having it confirmed was the last thing she needed right now.

'He's not my mark,' she said. Cristiano merely looked disbelieving. 'You have no right to judge me,' she snapped, her nerves strung tight. Cristiano was hardly the person to be angry with, but no one else was available, and frankly she could use a tiny bit of sympathy right then. 'So what do you suggest I do?'

'Lie low for a while,' Cristiano stated carelessly, as if it was all of very little concern to him. And, of course, it was. She might have been semi-cyber-stalking him for the last ten years but Laurel very much doubted he'd given her so much as a thought. She was half-amazed he'd even remembered her name.

'Lie low,' she repeated, and she was the disbelieving one now. 'How? And where? I left my handbag in his hotel suite and all my belongings are back in the *pensione*.' She drew a quick, sharp breath. 'Will you *please* send someone to fetch them? It's a small favour…'

'A small favour? I'm hardly about to send one of my staff into a very difficult situation, *bella*.'

'Don't call me that,' she returned tightly. She knew he didn't mean it and it felt mocking. A sneer she couldn't stand when she already felt scraped raw, everything about this situation making her feel intensely, painfully vulnerable.

'Why not?' Cristiano challenged, his voice turning soft, seductive. 'You are very beautiful. I am merely stating fact.' His gaze lingered, caressing her, making her respond. She felt heat unfurl in her belly and pool between her thighs, a treacherous and most inconvenient heat she was doing her best to deny.

'Why is it difficult?' she persisted, trying to pretend he wasn't affecting her. That a blush wasn't sweeping in a scorching tidal wave over her entire body.

'Because Bavasso is an unpleasant man and he is likely to make things difficult for anyone who helps someone who thwarted him. I have no doubt he will have his security detail waiting at your hotel. If someone shows up asking for your room key, they'll know.'

'But couldn't you…couldn't someone be discreet?'

Cristiano's eyes narrowed. 'You might feel entirely at ease with putting an innocent person in such a situation, but I am not.'

Laurel swayed as she was hit afresh by what an awful mess she'd managed to get herself into. Feeling as if her legs might give way beneath her, she walked to the sofa across from Cristiano and sank onto it. 'What am I going to do?' she whispered, more to herself than to Cristiano. She dropped her head into her hands and closed her eyes. 'What am I going to *do*?'

Cristiano suppressed the pang of sympathy he felt for Laurel. The sight of her sitting there with her head in her hands, her hair falling in a golden-brown water-fall around her face, her robe gaping open to reveal slender, golden thighs… What man wouldn't be affected? Not just by sympathy, but by desire. He suppressed that too. It was inconvenient at the moment, although he'd noted Laurel's obvious response to him with interest. He'd also noted her attempt to cover it. For whatever reason, she didn't want him knowing how he affected her, and she hadn't made any attempt to ask to stay, so what game was she playing?

'The answer seems fairly obvious,' he remarked as he strolled to the window and gazed out at the view of Rome's skyline by night. 'You stay here.'

He glanced back at Laurel; she raised her head, her aquamarine eyes wide with shock, the exact colour of the sunlit Aegean Sea. Her hair hung in damp ringlets around her heart-shaped face and her robe—his robe, actually—had slid off one shoulder, revealing its perfect curve.

'Stay here?' She frowned, her expression of confusion almost comical and definitely suspect. She was putting it on quite thickly for his benefit, and why? This was surely what she'd wanted. What she'd been hoping for. He was a far better bet than Bavasso. So did she think her reluctance would somehow earn her brownie points or, heaven help him, trust?

He trusted no one, especially not a woman like Laurel Forrester.

'Yes,' Cristiano answered, his voice clipped, touched with impatience. 'Stay here.'

'For how long?'

'As long as is necessary.' He paused, letting his gaze sweep over her once more. The robe gaped at her chest and he could see the shadowy vee between her breasts, almost glimpse their sweet, apple-like curves. 'As long as I want you to stay.' She drew in a quick, sharp breath, colour flooding her face. She almost looked outraged. 'You don't need to look quite so bewildered,' Cristiano drawled.

'Why shouldn't I be bewildered?' Laurel demanded. 'It almost sounded as if…'

'As if what?' Cristiano prompted silkily. She bit her lip and looked away.

'Nothing.'

Cristiano almost laughed at that. She didn't want to overplay her hand. She was so obvious, it amused him. Almost. The trouble was, he hated game playing. All his liaisons had been conducted with discretion and honesty, from their businesslike beginning to the expected end of the transaction. This would be no different, but he'd humour her for a little while… just to see where she'd go with this. What exactly she was trying to get? How much?

'So how long would that be?' Laurel asked, straightening as she drew the robe closed at her throat, every inch the outraged virgin. 'Because I don't even have any clothes.'

'A day or two at most. Bavasso will have moved on by then, no doubt.' He let his gaze linger. 'As for clothes… I'm not at all sure they'll be necessary.' She gasped and he laughed. 'Relax, *bella*. I'm only joking.' Sort of. 'I'll arrange for some clothes to be brought up to you.'

'Thank you,' she said stiffly and looked away. Cristiano propped one shoulder against the floor-to-ceiling window, taking the time to study her. The puppyish roundness of her teenage years had melted away, leaving behind a lithe yet curvaceous body. She was slender, verging on petite, yet her legs seemed endless and golden, her hair a cascade of colours, from chestnut brown to tawny orange to pure gold. She must pay her hairdresser a fortune.

'So where is home, out of interest?' he asked. 'Since it's obviously not Rome.'

She darted him a quick, suspicious glance before answering, 'Illinois.'

'Illinois?' That surprised him, although he knew she and her mother were American. His father had picked up Elizabeth Forrester in a third-rate casino in Miami and had married her just four days later. 'Chicago?' He would have expected Los Angeles or New York, somewhere where she could be seen and admired—and where she could find a sugar daddy.

'No, a small town you've never heard of.' Her tone was repressive. 'Are you going to order those clothes?'

'You're being quite demanding, for a woman who has nothing to offer… Unless you do have something to offer?' He intentionally let a note of innuendo into his voice and saw how her pupils flared in response. This was so *easy*.

'My gratitude,' Laurel bit out. She turned her head away, refusing to look at him.

'Ah, well, the question remains, how is one's gratitude expressed?' He enjoyed toying with her, enjoyed the way her breasts rose and fell with every agitated breath. A rosy blush swept across her collarbone. She had the most delectable skin, all golden cream and roses. He couldn't wait to touch it. Taste it.

'I would hope a simple thank you would do.' In one

abrupt movement she rose from the sofa, pulling the huge robe more tightly around her slender frame. 'I don't understand you, Cristiano. An hour ago I was attacked. Why are you toying with me like this? Do you enjoy being cruel?'

Annoyance sparked. 'You call this cruel?' He took a step closer to her, noting the gold sparks in her eyes, as well as the ones firing between them. 'How, *bella*, am I toying with you?'

'You know.' She kept her face averted, her breath coming in quick, ragged bursts. She didn't want to say it. Admit it. And Cristiano realised he very much wanted her to.

'I don't know, actually. I need you to enlighten me.'

She drew a tortured breath, looking anywhere but at him. 'Fine. You're almost sounding as if…as if you expect me to…something to happen between us.'

'Something is already happening between us, *bella*,' Cristiano answered softly. 'Can't you feel it?' He certainly could. He felt it in the tautening of the air, the heightened awareness he had of her: of every draw and tear of her breathing; the pearly sheen of her skin; the way his loins tightened when she touched her lips with her tongue.

'I just want to go home,' she said, her voice low. 'This isn't my world. I don't belong here.'

'You were certainly acting as if you belonged here earlier in the evening.'

Finally she looked at him, horrified realisation and hurt flashing in her aquamarine eyes. 'You saw…?'

'I saw everything. You on the casino floor with Rico Bavasso—practically sitting in his lap, laughing at his jokes, letting him paw you while your mother watched. She taught you well, I suppose.'

She shook her head, curls bouncing. 'It wasn't like that…'

'It was exactly like that and you know it,' he answered, a hint of steel entering his voice. 'Now what I'm wondering is, why are you acting like an outraged virgin now?'

She let out a cry and whirled away, stalking towards the lift doors. Cristiano watched her, darkly amused, as she pushed the button.

'You intend to go down to the lobby, to face Rico Bavasso and his security, in my dressing gown? Because that is not a tactic I'd recommend you employ. It will end badly for you. Very badly indeed.'

'I'll take my chances,' she said, her whole body taut and quivering, his robe trailing the ground.

'That's quite a risk you're willing to take, then.'

'And one I prefer.'

Her games were getting tiresome. What on earth did she possibly hope to gain from them? She had his interest already. Playing hard to get, or as if she were some offended innocent, was both pointless and aggravating. 'Unfortunately it's one I do not prefer,' Cristiano said lazily. 'The lift is locked, *bella*. You're not going anywhere. Not until I say so.'

CHAPTER THREE

LAUREL WHIRLED AROUND, the breath leaving her lungs in one almighty whoosh. Cristiano lounged against the window, his hands in his pockets, looking for all the world as if he were out for a summer stroll. Not as if he'd just threatened her. Not as if he'd just intimated that she was as captive in this hotel suite as she would be in Rico Bavasso's.

'Out of the frying pan and into the fire, it seems,' she managed, trying to keep her voice from shaking. Cristiano was not hiding the heat that simmered in his eyes, but she could hardly believe it. Ten years ago he'd batted her away like an annoying inconvenience. So now he wanted her, and she had no say in the matter?

'Fire has much to recommend it.'

She stared at him, caught between confusion and outrage. Was he teasing her? She couldn't believe that he wanted her badly enough now to keep her captive in his penthouse. She couldn't believe he wanted her at all. He had his pick of the most beautiful and glamorous women in the world, and she was an inexperienced hick from nowhere, Illinois. What could he possibly see in her?

'What do you want, Cristiano?' she asked slowly, not entirely sure she wanted to hear the answer.

He lifted his chin, his silver-grey eyes blazing, but with ice. Cold and hot at the same time—but didn't it feel like a burn, when you touched something icy and incredibly cold? That was how Cristiano felt to her. A cold blaze of danger.

'It's simple,' he said. 'I want you.'

He couldn't put it more plainly than that, yet still she was sceptical. 'Why me? You could have any woman you wanted.'

'Thank you.'

'Why should either of us pretend otherwise? You're in the celebrity gossip magazines often enough.'

'Why, *bella*, are you keeping tabs on me?'

'It would be hard not to, considering how often you feature in the press—and *please* don't call me *bella*.'

'All right. Laurel.' He spoke quietly, with a sincerity she hadn't heard before, his tone of voice low and heartfelt, affecting her in a way that his barely leashed looks had not. That tone left her feeling unsteady. Uncertain. And, shamefully, wanting.

'Well?' she demanded unsteadily. 'Why?'

'Why do I want you?'

'Yes.' She could hardly believe they were having this conversation. Cristiano's tone made it sound as if he were chatting about the weather.

'Why not?' Cristian answered with a shrug.

'That's it? "Why not"?' She stared at him, trying to fathom what was going on behind that inscrutable face, the negligent shrug of his powerful shoulders. Was it simply that a woman was available, a woman who he obviously assumed made free with her body, so of whom he intended to take advantage? The thought made her feel physically sick.

'You take issue with my response?' he enquired.

'Yes. You're practically threatening me—'

'There are no threats, Laurel.' Cristiano's voice cut across her, quick, lethal and very, very sure. 'Nothing I have said or done is a threat. And nothing will be.'

She flung one arm towards the lift doors. 'And the locked doors?'

'The last thing you want is for anyone to have free access to my flat.'

'Because of Bavasso?'

'I believe you underestimate him. Admittedly, he is able to turn on the charm when he wishes, but he can be a vicious man.'

She suppressed a shudder as she recalled Bavasso's hands on her, reaching, grabbing. 'I believe you,' she said. 'But I still don't appreciate feeling like a prisoner.'

'For your own safety, as well as my own, I must take precautions. I'm sure you understand.'

He was so smooth, so aggravatingly assured, that Laurel felt her protests falling away, unspoken. Cristiano had locked the doors, yet here she was, the one who felt as though she was being unreasonable.

'And if I insist on leaving?' she asked. 'What then?'

Cristiano shook his head slowly, his expression one of patently mock regret. 'But you see, I could not live with putting a woman into potential danger on my conscience. Especially one I was once, however happenstance, related to.'

'We were never related.'

He inclined his head in a regal nod. 'It is as you

say, of course. Stepsiblings hardly count as blood relations.'

'And surely you exaggerate?' Laurel persisted. She had to believe that. 'Rico Bavasso isn't *that* dangerous.' When she'd first met him, he'd seemed charming, just as Cristiano had said: silver-haired, hazel-eyed, all smooth urbanity. Admittedly something about his assured manner had made Laurel uneasy, but her mother had seemed happy, and Laurel had just wanted her money. Shame licked through her again at the thought.

Cristiano dropped his expression of fake regret as his gaze turned startlingly serious. 'Do you really want to take such a risk?'

Wordlessly Laurel shook her head. Bavasso had been so angry. She had no desire to run into him again, especially not any time soon.

'How well do you know him?' Cristiano asked. His voice was mild, even friendly, but with a ripple of darkness underneath that nearly made Laurel gulp again.

'I don't know him,' she said quickly. 'That is, not very well at all.' She didn't really want to go into the how and why of her acquaintance with Rico Bavasso, yet it seemed Cristiano had already assumed the absolute worst.

Which wasn't all that far from the truth, unfortunately—yet it felt different. It was different, at least to her. She hadn't thought Bavasso had been interested in *her*.

'You seemed as if you knew him quite well while you were on his lap, whispering in his ear,' Cristiano said in that same awful, mild tone.

'I wasn't on his lap,' she snapped.

'Close enough.'

Laurel shook her head. 'It wasn't what it looked like.'

'Funny, I think it was exactly what it looked like.'

'You would.' Clearly Cristiano was going to think the worst of her. And Laurel knew it had looked bad. How could she explain that she had never meant to lead Bavasso astray; that when he'd started cosying up to her she'd frozen inside, appalled and uncertain? And, with her mother smiling and nodding the whole while, she'd assumed it was all in her head, that she was being paranoid and oversensitive. If only.

'I believe you, as a matter of interest,' Cristiano drawled. 'I don't think you know him well. If you had, you would not have tangled with him so precipitously.'

'No, I wouldn't have,' Laurel agreed. Had her mother known what Bavasso was capable of? Had she been in on it? Had she realised that, if Laurel had known what Bavasso really wanted, she never would have agreed to set foot in all of Italy, much less a ca-sino in Rome? Cristiano's casino. 'Can I have some clothes, please?' Her voice sounded high and thin, as if she was scared.

And she was scared—of everything, at the moment. Scared of a future she couldn't even begin to fathom, a freedom she longed to grasp but which felt further away than ever. But she wasn't, Laurel realised, ac-tually scared of Cristiano. Despite his determination, his desire, she believed him. She had to believe him, believe that he wouldn't threaten or force her to do something she didn't want to do.

But the trouble was, he wouldn't be forcing her. Already she felt a dark, honeyed ribbon of longing wind its way through her, melting her resistance. Already she was imagining the feel of his lips on hers. Already she was anticipating the delicious, icy burn of his touch. His caress.

'Of course you can have some clothes,' Cristiano answered smoothly, thankfully distracting her from her fevered imaginings. 'As a matter of fact, I already ordered them while you were in the shower. You seem to think I am some sort of brute, Laurel, which I confess I find a bit ironic, considering the man you just fled. I hope the contrast between us is more than apparent.'

It was. Oh, it was. Laurel didn't trust herself to answer so she turned away, walking towards the windows, taking in the incredible view.

She heard Cristiano move and then she felt him come up behind her. Her breath froze in her lungs and her heart felt suspended in her chest. Every nerve was strung tight, every sense on overload. And he wasn't even touching her.

Then Cristiano laid a hand on her shoulder. Even through the thick terrycloth robe she felt the press of his palm like a brand, a burn, and it took everything she had not to respond—although she didn't even know how she would. Move closer or further away? Her body would betray her.

'I should tell you now,' he said in a soft voice, 'That I abhor game playing of any kind. Every transaction I've had with a woman has been straightforward and intensely pleasurable. So, if you think you can gain something more from me than what I have already offered by playing the coy miss, think again.'

He squeezed her shoulder lightly, a warning, while

Laurel's mind spun. Everything he'd said was offensive, appalling. She didn't even know how to begin to respond. A transaction? Intensely pleasurable? Coy miss? She nearly choked with affront at it all.

'What exactly are you offering?' she finally asked in a shaky voice when she'd managed to kick her mind back into gear and could form at least one coherent sentence. 'Out of curiosity?'

At last, a straightforward question. And he would give a straightforward response. Finally they were getting somewhere.

'My protection,' Cristiano said as he stepped away from her, deciding he needed a little space to stay cool and level-headed. When he'd been standing behind her he'd inhaled her scent, something light and fresh, a hint of lemon and violets. He'd felt her heat, warm and seductive, and the desire to slip the robe from her shoulders and feel the silky skin underneath had been so strong his palms had itched. His body had ached.

'Your protection?' she repeated. He couldn't quite gauge her tone, veering between tremulous and infuriated.

'From Bavasso.'

She stayed where she stood, staring out at the darkness, a slight, slender figure swathed in dark blue. 'Do I really need protection?'

'For a short time, yes.'

'And how can you protect me? By keeping me here?'

'Initially, yes. Bavasso is like a child with a toy when it comes to women. The best way to get him

to forget you is for you to be seen to belong to someone else.' He paused, waiting for that to sink in, then
continued, 'Bavasso enjoys the use of my hotels and
casinos. If he discovers that you are with me, he will
not pursue you.' Bavasso was a vicious man, but only
with those weaker than him. Cristiano was confident
Bavasso would not bother with Laurel once he realised
she was off-limits. And he very much intended her to
be off-limits…to anyone but him.

'*With* you?' Laurel's jaw hardened, her mouth set
in a line as she continued to stare out into the night.
'Is that a euphemism?'

'It is fact.' Their affair was only a matter of time.
Surely she realised that? Surely she felt it in the desire
that shimmered and pulsed between them, an energy
force neither of them could deny?

'And so I exchange one man's unwanted attention
for another.' She spoke flatly and Cristiano prickled
with irritation. He did not believe his attention was
so *unwanted*.

'Again you are comparing me with Bavasso, and I
will remind you of the contrast.'

'Oh, you're certainly more attractive,' Laurel said
as she turned around, true bitterness spiking her
words. 'I'll grant you that. Although, Bavasso is good-
looking in that "silver fox" kind of way.' She tossed
the words out, but beneath the blaze of anger he felt
they'd cost her. 'And your…seduction would no doubt
be far more assured and deft,' she added. 'But it still
amounts to the same thing.'

'It does not.' His whole body was twanging with
both indignation and awareness. How dared she compare him to sly, sleek Bavasso? And how could he

want her now, more than ever, when she was verbally repelling him as best she could?

Laurel lifted her chin, her eyes flashing blue-green fire. 'Tell me how it doesn't, then.'

Cristiano stared at her for a long moment, his jaw clenched, fists too. He felt angry, aware and *wanting*. 'I told you before, I do not threaten. I certainly do not force. Trust me on that, Laurel.'

'Why should I trust you on anything?' she challenged. 'And, in any case, there are different kinds of coercion.' She looked away, a flush staining her cheeks, her teeth sinking provocatively into her full lower lip. Realisation dawned and bloomed inside him, making him smile. She wasn't afraid of him forcing her. She was afraid she wouldn't need to be forced.

'Coercion?' he asked softly. 'Or seduction?'

She drew a shuddering breath, lifting her chin and tossing her hair back, forcing herself to meet his knowing gaze. Because he did know—he knew that she wanted him, just as he wanted her. Why she was fighting the attraction, however, remained a mystery. Was she holding out for more? 'What else do you offer?' she asked. 'Besides protection?'

'Pleasure.' He watched her eyes flare, but to her credit she held his gaze. 'Of that you can be certain.'

'You are appallingly arrogant.'

'Merely sure.'

She shook her head slowly. 'And how long would this…arrangement between us last?'

'As long as I want it to.' He felt the first flickers of triumph, mingled with a strange and unsettling disappointment. After all her maidenly outrage, Laurel was acting exactly as he'd expected her to, needed her to…and he found he didn't quite like it.

'And how long would that be, do you think?' she asked. Her eyes flashed and her lips trembled, fury and fear mingled together. 'Judging from what I've read in the tabloids, your mistresses don't last more than a week. And we are talking about me becoming your mistress, aren't we? That's the position I'm being interviewed for, isn't it?'

'Call it what you like.' He'd had straightforward discussions with previous mistresses, but for some reason they hadn't felt quite like this: so cold and mercenary. Although, mercenary was exactly how he'd always wanted to be, especially when it came to women. Any softer emotion, never mind actual love, was for fools. Fools like his father, who had been both fleeced and heartbroken by grasping women like Laurel's mother and the wife before her. As for his own mother…

'So for how long?' she asked, a catch in her voice. 'Roughly?'

Cristiano's eyes narrowed. 'For as long as it takes for Bavasso to be satisfied that you're off-limits.' And as long as he still wanted her.

'It's my safety you're thinking of, is it?'

Now he was getting seriously irritated. 'Among other things.'

'How kind of you,' she drawled, and he could not mistake her sarcasm. He watched her walk across the room, the sash of his robe trailing the ground, her long, wavy hair cascading over her shoulders. She looked like a young, hesitant queen and, in spite of everything, or perhaps because of it, for a moment he admired her.

'Your safety is important to me,' he said, 'whether you believe it or not.'

'Why should it be? I doubt you even thought of me once in the last ten years.'

'Then you thought wrong.'

She stilled at his tone, which was quieter and more sincere than he'd meant it to be. 'Any thoughts you've had of me can't have been good ones,' she said, her tone as quiet as his, and equally sincere. 'Can they?'

'Some were…interesting.'

'Interesting?' She turned around to face him. 'I thought you might despise me, Cristiano.'

'*Despise* is a strong word.'

'Your father despises my mother.'

'I am not my father and you are not your mother.'

'No.' She drew a quick breath. 'But you've judged me just as you've judged her. Tarred us both with the same brush.'

'And I have had obvious reason to do so. Are you telling me differently?'

She looked away. 'You wouldn't listen.'

Cristiano could not imagine any scenario that could excuse or explain her behaviour with Bavasso on the casino floor. 'I'd listen,' he said mildly, 'but whether I believed you or not is another matter. In any case, why do you care what I think of you? Emotions have no place here, *bella*. This is about something else entirely. Something basic and very, very pleasurable.' He started walking towards her slowly, and she stilled, trapped, mesmerised by his lazy yet purposeful words.

Perhaps now it was time to show her just how pleasurable it all could be.

'You paint such an appealing picture,' Laurel said huskily. She didn't move. 'No emotions, no concern for feelings, just sex. For maybe a week.'

'Sounds perfect to me.' He kept walking until he was standing right in front of her. She hadn't budged, and he knew he had her. 'Stop playing your games,' he whispered as he reached for the sash of her robe—*his* robe—and tugged her towards him. She came, reluctantly, perhaps, but her pointless act of protest was already being revealed as the masquerade he'd known it was. Her hips nudged his and heat flared bright and white-hot inside him. He sucked in a hard breath and tugged again at the sash. Her eyes widened as she felt the evidence of his arousal.

He touched her chin with one fingertip, tilting her face to his. 'This can really be very simple.'

'To you.'

'And to you. Why not?' He stroked her cheek and she closed her eyes. A shudder went through her. 'See how you respond to me?' he murmured. 'And I haven't even kissed you yet.' He stroked her cheek again, enjoying the silky feel of her skin, the tremor that went through her whole body. 'We are going to be very, very good together, *bella*. I feel it. I know it.'

She let out a shuddering gasp and then opened her eyes, wrenching herself away from him as if she had to break steel bonds to be free. Her eyes shot bluegreen sparks at him as she clutched the gaping robe together with one hand.

'What I know, Cristiano, is that you're an arrogant, manipulative bastard and I have no intention of making any sort of deal with you, now or ever. So why don't you practise your so-called charms on some other woman who wants them?' With another gasp that sounded halfway to a sob, she turned from the room and ran down the hall, slamming the bedroom door behind him and then turning the lock with an audible click.

CHAPTER FOUR

LAUREL FELT AS if she needed another shower. She paced Cristiano's bedroom, her heart racing, her whole body tingling despite the storm of indignation raging through her. No matter what big words she'd just thrown at him, she'd been tempted—seriously tempted—and for one glorious second she'd been sure he was going to kiss her, had imagined the sensuous slide of his lips along hers...

What was happening to her? How had she fallen down this rabbit hole of manipulation, sex and greed? She lived a quiet life in a small town in Illinois, working as a nurse, possessing a handful of casual friends, and no boyfriends, ever. For a second she pictured her grandfather's farmhouse—its floorboards of weathered, honeyed oak, the view of rolling fields from the kitchen window, the friendly glimmer of the pond in the distance. She ached to go home, for things to feel familiar and safe again. Boring, even. She didn't want this. She didn't want any of this—not her mother, not Bavasso, not Cristiano.

Liar.

She silenced that taunting inner voice by sheer strength of will and tried to think practically about what she should do now, since she seemed intent on burning her bridges both left and right.

She couldn't leave Cristiano's penthouse, not yet anyway. She took his warning about Bavasso seriously…just as she took his offer of no-strings sex seriously.

Why wouldn't you become the man's mistress?

Frustration bubbled inside her and she paced the room, feeling both frantic and caged. She wouldn't become the man's mistress because she had more self-respect than that. More pride. And more of an instinct of self-preservation. Sex with Cristiano would burn her up, leaving nothing but cinders. She felt that in her very bones, knew it from the way she'd reacted to his hand on her shoulder, the merest brush of his hips against hers…

Heat flared through her at that potent memory and she whirled away from the window, pacing the room to the bathroom and back. At this rate she'd wear out the thick pile carpet.

A knock sounded on the door and she stilled, every muscle tense, every sense on high-octane alert. 'Yes?'

'Your clothes have arrived.'

She couldn't tell anything from Cristiano's tone. Warily Laurel opened the door. He stood there, one hand outstretched with several luxury shopping bags dangling from his long, lean fingers.

'Thank you,' Laurel said stiffly, taking the bags. 'You didn't have to get so much.'

'Who knows how long you will be here, *bella*?' Cristiano answered lazily.

'Not very long, if I can help it,' Laurel retorted. 'I'm going to get dressed and then we need to talk.'

'Excellent. I've ordered some food, so we can talk as we eat.'

It all suddenly seemed so civilised, Laurel thought with a savage twist of humour as she closed the door. Almost as if Cristiano wasn't keeping her captive, intending for her to be his mistress. To keep her here for *sex*. It seemed ridiculous, laughable, yet she felt the seriousness of the situation all the way through her body, right down to her toes.

She emptied the bags on the bed, blinking at the sight of the elegant clothes, which included several outfits, including undergarments. How on earth had he managed to know her bra size? she wondered as she picked up a push-up bra in nude lace and coffee-coloured satin. Although, on second thoughts, Cristiano no doubt could gauge a woman's bra size from across a crowded room.

She chose the most conservative outfit, a swishy knee-length skirt in pale blue and a matching silk T-shirt top. Now that she was finally dressed in something that was neither revealing nor inappropriate, she felt a little more restored to herself. Almost as if the last seventy hours had never happened. Almost, but not quite.

In addition to the clothes, Cristiano had thoughtfully provided a bag of luxury toiletries, and Laurel took advantage of them, putting on a little discreet make-up, brushing her hair and twisting it up into a knot.

Taking a deep breath, she headed out of the bedroom. She found Cristiano in the dining area on the far side of the living room setting out food on a table that looked as if it had been carved from a single piece of ebony.

Laurel inhaled the tantalising scents of basil and lemon, and realised she hadn't eaten anything since lunch. All evening Bavasso had plied her with cocktails she'd tried not to drink and no food.

Her stomach growled audibly and Cristiano looked up, humour glinting in those silvery eyes. Laurel managed a little laugh. 'I'm hungry.'

'So I hear.' He gestured to one of the chairs, made of gleaming black wood. 'Come sit down.'

Laurel hesitated, discomfited by this apparently new normal. Then she decided she would take what civility Cristiano offered, and she slid a chair out and sat down as he lifted the silver domes off several dishes.

'What would you like?' Cristiano asked as he lifted a plate. Laurel glanced at all the different dishes of Italian specialities, from *fiore di zucca*, a Roman dish of courgette fritters, to pasta carbonara and several delicious-looking salads.

'It all looks good to me.'

'Then I shall give you a bit of everything.'

Laurel watched as he ladled the different dishes onto her plate, feeling as if she'd fallen down yet another rabbit hole. Why had Cristiano changed his tune so drastically? Why was he being so *nice*?

'Thank you,' she murmured as she took her plate from him. Cristiano filled up his own and sat down on the opposite end of the table.

'Dig in,' he said in the same mild tone he'd been using since she'd emerged from the bedroom. 'I'm glad the clothes fit,' he said with a nod to her skirt and top. 'That colour of blue was a good choice. It brings out your eyes.'

'Um, thank you?'

He arched a dark eyebrow. 'Can you not accept a compliment?'

'It just sounded…' Laurel hesitated, wondering if she was being hypersensitive. 'Proprietary.'

'Proprietary?' His smile and eyes both gleamed. 'About you or the clothes?'

'Both.'

Cristiano sat back in his chair. 'Stop fighting it, *bella*,' he said, his tone turning lazy. 'It would be far more pleasant for both of us if you did.'

'Stop fighting it? Or you?'

'Both.'

They stared at each other, a stand-off, and one that made fireworks fizz in Laurel's middle. There could be no mistaking the, yes, *proprietary* gleam in Cristiano's silvery-grey gaze. And definitely not just about the clothes. But, instead of feeling outraged and objectified as she knew she should, Laurel felt…excited.

Excited to know the heat simmering in those silvery depths was for her. She might be no more than a convenience, the expedient option, but he still wanted her. And, Bavasso's odious groping aside, Laurel had precious little experience with being wanted.

So why *was* she fighting it? Her body battled with her brain, with both sense and self-preservation. The look stretched and lengthened between them and Laurel fought to hold onto all the reasons why she should not engage in some temporary, tasteless affair with Cristiano Ferrero.

Because this was his world, not hers, and she was already out of her depth. Because she had enough experience of people who loved and then left you, starting with her own parents—as well as Cristiano's father, Lorenzo. She didn't need another reminder. Because she was too innocent, too naïve, and too darn hopeful to survive the kind of arrangement Cristiano was suggesting.

Because he was dangerous, as dangerous as holding a firework in your hand and letting yourself be mesmerised by the fizz and spark. It wouldn't take long for it to blow up in your face. To ruin your life.

Laurel dragged her gaze away from Cristiano's simmering, steady one. 'I want to ask about my mother,' she said when she trusted her voice to sound normal. Her body was still reacting, little electric pulses going off in the strangest of places. Low in her belly. Between her thighs.

'Your mother?' Oh, that mild, enquiring tone. Already she knew to suspect it.

'Yes. If Rico Bavasso is as unpleasant as you say, then I'm worried for her.'

'*Bella*, if there's one thing I know, it's that your mother can take of herself.'

Laurel glanced up sharply. 'What's that supposed to mean?'

'Let's not pretend when it comes to your mother,' Cristiano answered. Gone was that mild tone, replaced by something far harder. Something that hinted at the unrelenting steel she knew lurked beneath his smooth urbanity. 'We both know what she is.'

'Which is?' Laurel threw at him. She wasn't under any illusions about what Cristiano Ferrero or his father thought of her mother, but some perverse, de-termined streak in her still wanted to hear him say it out loud.

'She is a craven, amoral, shameless, gold-digging liar,' Cristiano stated with flat and final authority. Laurel opened her mouth but nothing came out. She hadn't expected him to state it quite so plainly. So coldly. 'And,' he continued, 'I have no reason not to think you are the same.'

Cristiano watched the colour drain from Laurel's face and wished he didn't feel guilty for speaking so plainly. Aggravatingly, at every step it seemed he had to remind himself to act in the manner to which he'd become accustomed—matter-of-fact to the point of ruthlessness.

Anything else smacked of weakness or want and was completely unacceptable. He would never suc-cumb to either option, as his mother did, or manipu-lation and lies, as his father did, letting himself get ensnared in a sticky web of a woman's deceit.

No man was an island, but he was doing his damnedest to try. But Laurel didn't have to look so *wounded*. As if he'd sucker-punched her when he'd been stating the obvious.

'Well.' Her voice was shaky as she placed her nap-kin next to her plate of barely touched food. 'Don't sugar-coat it.'

'I see no need to sugar-coat anything,' Cristiano replied shortly. 'Surely we are both aware of the facts surrounding our parents' divorce?'

'If you mean, did Lorenzo Ferrero cut my mother and me out of his life without so much as a goodbye, then yes, I'm aware.' A bright spot of colour appeared on each glorious cheekbone, enflaming and annoying him in turns.

'You almost sound as if you were the one who was betrayed.'

'I was.' Laurel pressed her lips together, as if she'd revealed too much with that statement. She looked away, blinking hard. 'But clearly you don't think I have any right to that feeling. Clearly you think, even without knowing me at all, that I am one step up from a prostitute.'

For a second Cristiano paused. He could see Laurel was battling intense emotion, and he didn't think she was faking it. 'I accept that you were young at the time of our parents' divorce,' he said after a moment. 'You might not have been aware of your mother's actions.'

'And yet you said you judged me as you judged her,' Laurel returned. Her lips were white, her eyes huge, the only colour in her face those two bright spots.

'I said I had no reason to think you were different. Prove me wrong if you can.'

'Why should I bother?' she flung back at him. 'You're…you're disgusting.' She rose from the table, her body taut and trembling. 'You disgust me. You act so superior, as if you're standing above everyone, judging their actions when you have no clue, no *concept*, of what our lives are really like. And meanwhile your actions are just as reprehensible as my mother's, or even those of Rico Bavasso.'

'Don't compare me to that man,' Cristiano warned in a low voice.

'Why shouldn't I? You trapped me here—'

'I rescued you.'

'You propositioned me and still you refuse to let me go. At least I managed to escape Bavasso's clutches.' She shook her head, her lip curling in genuine disgust. She was *repulsed* by him. The realisation was shocking and deeply, deeply unsettling. For the first time Cristiano didn't wonder what game she was playing, but whether she was playing one at all. And right now he didn't think she was. He'd been trying to get her to be honest, and it seemed he'd succeeded in that goal. It just hadn't turned out at all as he'd expected.

'Your mother doesn't matter to me,' he said swiftly. 'We never should have talked about her in the first place. She is not relevant to our discussions.'

'We talked about her because I'm worried for her safety, no matter what you think of her or her actions of ten years ago. Can you please see that she is all right? Regardless of what you think of her, surely you have that much honour?'

Elizabeth Forrester had always struck Cristiano as the kind of woman who knew exactly on which side her bread was buttered, but for Laurel's sake he nodded tersely. 'Very well.'

'Thank you.'

A truce, then, of sorts. Laurel glanced down at her plate and then, her chin tilted at a haughty, proud angle, she sat down and started to eat again. It seemed Laurel Forrester knew on which side her bread was buttered as well.

'How did you feel betrayed by my father?' Cristiano asked abruptly. The remark had niggled at him.

Laurel looked up warily. 'Because one minute we were all playing happy families, and the next my mother and I were on the plane back to Illinois, and I never even saw him again. Not so much as a text.'

'And your mother had two million euros in her private bank account,' Cristiano reminded her flatly.

'Two million euros that your father got back,' Laurel retorted. 'Thanks to his water-tight pre-nup agreement. She didn't see a penny of it.'

'That makes it better, then? Just because she was caught?'

Laurel had the grace to look away. 'Caught doing what, exactly?' she hedged. Did she think he didn't know?

'Caught stealing from my father,' he snapped, annoyed that she was practically defending her mother's indefensible actions. 'Taking his money and squirreling it away.'

'Is it stealing, when they were married?' Laurel asked quietly. 'She took money from a joint bank account. Technically it was hers too.'

'Technically,' Cristiano agreed, the word bitten off and spit out. 'Fortunately the law did not consider it a technicality.'

'Still,' Laurel persisted. 'What's yours is mine and vice versa, isn't that right? Or do you not believe in marriage vows?'

Cristiano sat back, starting to fume. He really hadn't wanted to rake up old memories of Elizabeth Forrester's betrayal of his father, but Laurel was forcing his hand. 'She was stealing from him, *bella*, no question.'

'I admit it might have *looked* like that, but she didn't mean it the way you—'

'She was siphoning money from various accounts

and putting it in an offshore account under a different name!' Cristiano cut her off, his voice like the snick of a blade. 'Are you actually defending her?'

'Not defending,' Laurel answered, a flush rising to her face. 'I know she's…' She stopped and shook her head, clearly at a loss, because she couldn't defend her mother even if she wanted to. Elizabeth Forrester was so clearly indefensible.

'And what was that money for?' Cristiano continued, relentless now. 'The day when she left him for some toy boy? Considering her behaviour since then, it seems likely.'

Laurel's face went pale again. 'What do you know of my mother's behaviour since then?'

'Tonight was not the first time she has come into La Sirena.' He didn't make a point of following Elizabeth Forrester's romantic entanglements, but he'd seen her enough times over the last ten years—usually on the arm of some puffed-up aristo, fawning, flirting and making Cristiano nauseous—to know that she lived by her wits and fading beauty. Every time he'd seen her he'd felt vindicated in telling his father about the private account he'd discovered ten years ago.

'Tonight was the first time I came into La Sirena,' Laurel said quietly. 'Or had that escaped your notice?'

Cristiano stared at her, trying to decipher what she was really trying to say. That she was different from her mother? Or perhaps just more discreet. 'So why did you?' he asked. 'Out of interest?'

He waited, bracing himself for some spun-out sob story about desperate times and hard circumstances. But she just pursed her lips and shook her head. 'It doesn't matter.'

And Cristiano told himself that was fine, because it didn't. He wasn't interested in getting to know Laurel, yet against his better judgment, and all common sense, he was curious. What had she been doing for the last ten years? Living the way her mother did? It was the utterly obvious assumption, and yet…

Something in him resisted that assumption, which was stupid as well as pointless. Laurel toyed with her fork and then pushed her plate away. 'I'm sorry. I'm not hungry any more.'

'You should eat.' She was slender enough for a breath to blow her away. She just shook her head.

'I… I think I'll go to bed. It's late and it's been a very long day. A very long couple of days.' She rose from the table, pausing uncertainly. 'Thank you,' she said. 'For the clothes and the food and the place to stay.'

As if he'd given it all to her out of the goodness of his heart. As if their arrangement, the one he still most definitely wanted, didn't remain on the table, needing to be discussed. Cristiano rose too.

'I'll see you to your room.'

Her pupils flared. 'That isn't necessary.'

'Oh, but I assure you,' he answered softly, 'It is.'

Laurel stared at him for a beat longer and then wordlessly turned from the room. Cristiano followed her to the door of his bedroom, where she hesitated, her back quivering with tension.

'Where…where am I to sleep?'

'There is a guest bedroom across the hall.' He pushed open the door opposite his own. She turned to glance at him, and that was her mistake. Her breath came out in a rush as heat flared between them. Cristiano put his hand on her wrist, felt the leap of her pulse beneath his fingers. Laurel pressed her lips together.

'Don't, Cristiano,' she whispered.

'Don't what?'

'Don't touch me.'

'Don't tempt you?' He stroked the silky skin of her inner wrist with his thumb. 'Is that what you mean?' He ran his thumb gently down to her palm and then up to her inner elbow. Laurel remained frozen, her pulse hammering beneath his questing fingers. 'Why deny what is between us, *bella*?'

'There's nothing between us.' She nearly had to gasp the words out.

'Your body begs to differ.'

'Ten years ago you shoved me away as if I disgusted you.'

'Ten years ago you were a child. What was I supposed to do?'

She turned to face him, her breast brushing his arm. 'Don't pretend you felt anything for me then.'

'The point is what I feel for you now. And what you feel for me. It's real, *bella*, what is between us. Why shouldn't we enjoy it?'

He could see the indecision in her fractured gaze, the desire as well as the doubt. All she needed was the tiniest bit of incentive, the merest push to tumble her into temptation...and he was more than willing to give it.

'Stop worrying so much,' he murmured as he dropped his head so his lips were a fraction away from hers. He could hear her breaths, uneven and ragged. 'What are you afraid of?' he added, his lips very nearly brushing hers.

'This,' she whispered, and then Cristiano kissed her.

CHAPTER FIVE

It FELT AS achingly wonderful as she could ever have imagined. Better. *Far* better. Sweet and dark at the same time, and so very intense. Cristiano was entirely in control, commanding her response. Demanding it.

Laurel's head fell back as Cristiano's lips moved on hers and he deepened the kiss, his tongue plundering the soft depths of her mouth, taking ownership, sending pulses of pleasure through her whole body.

It was just a kiss, yet it felt life-changing. Soul-shattering. He put his hand on her waist, his fingers splaying over the dip of her hip, his palm burning her through the thin silk of her skirt, another brand. In this moment he owned her and they both knew it.

Laurel couldn't have broken that kiss even if she'd wanted to, which, to her own shame, she did not. She craved his touch, the explosion of sensation inside her an excitement that was impossible to contain or deny, licking through her veins, making her stand on tiptoe to give him greater access, to reach more of him.

Cristiano pulled her to him, fitting her body intimately to his so need roared through her veins and heat flared deeper and hotter.

He kissed his way from her mouth to her neck, his

tongue teasing circles against her fevered skin; his hands stroking her hips, her thighs, making everything inside her coil so tightly. She felt as if she was about to explode, as if she needed to break apart. She arched against him, unable to help herself, her mind a haze of need as she craved the kind of release she'd never experienced with a man before.

Cristiano growled low in his throat and he skimmed his fingers underneath her skirt, running the tips along her inner thigh, teasing the sensitive skin before his thumb nudged the edge of her underwear and then slipped beneath, making her gasp at the shock of the tender invasion.

For a few blissful seconds Laurel couldn't even think. She'd never been touched so intimately, so knowingly. And with such expertise. Cristiano knew exactly how a few lazy strokes sent her spinning, all her muscles clenching, her nails digging into his shoulders, everything in her straining as she fought for both control and release. She couldn't have both—there was a battle raging inside her, and she didn't know which side she wanted to win.

Her eyes fluttered open and through the daze of desire she caught sight of her own reflection on the mirrored wall—her flushed face, her swollen lips, her half-lidded eyes, her arched hips. But as for Cristiano— he didn't look half as affected as she did. His expression was shuttered, his lips slightly pursed as he continued to touch her in such an intimate way. He looked almost clinical, dispassionate, a scientist conducting an experiment with guaranteed results. He was working her body. Manipulating her.

With a cry Laurel jerked out of his arms. Cristiano's startled gaze clashed with hers and his eyes narrowed.

'What…?'

'Don't,' she said raggedly. Her body pulsed with unfulfilled desire—and shame. She'd fallen right into his arms. Into his trap. 'Don't,' she said again, and stumbled into the bedroom, slamming the door in his face.

She flipped the lock, letting out a shuddering breath, her body still pulsing with pleasure—and frustration. Pushing her tangled hair away from her face, she paced the room that was just as sumptuous as Cristiano's own. What on earth was she going to do now?

Wait seemed like the only option. Laurel washed her face, combed her hair and then slumped into a leather armchair by the window overlooking the Tiber, gleaming in the moonlight. It had to be at least three in the morning, and her body ached with exhaustion, yet she knew she wouldn't be able to sleep. She tried to make her mind empty out, but it seethed with worries and memories. Bavasso's leering face. Her desperate flight. Cristiano's kiss.

She must have dozed off, because a knock on the door startled her awake. She'd been dreaming… dreaming of Cristiano. Hands…lips… Her body tingled as if he'd been touching her.

'Yes?' she called, her voice sounding hoarse and scratchy.

'I checked on your mother,' Cristiano called through the door, his voice gruff. 'She's all right.'

Laurel swallowed. 'Where is she?'

'She went back to the *pensione* where you were staying. Bavasso shouted at her, but that was all. It's you he's angry at, not her. Who knows? They might be able to patch things up.'

He spoke sardonically, and Laurel could hardly blame him. Bavasso wasn't the first boyfriend of her mother's to behave in a way that should have had Elizabeth sending him packing. Trouble was, if there was still something to be had, she never did.

'So he's still angry at me?' she asked after a tense pause.

'I'll take care of you, Laurel.'

The throb of sincerity in his voice shouldn't have affected her. Definitely shouldn't have made her eyes sting. 'I'm not sure I want to know what that means.'

'I won't let Bavasso bother or hurt you.'

But you'll hurt me, in an entirely different way. She thought of his cold, clinical face in the mirror. He'd known exactly what he'd been doing. Laurel blinked hard and didn't reply. 'Get some sleep,' Cristiano said roughly. 'It's nearly dawn. We'll talk later.'

'Okay.' A moment passed, silent, endless. Somehow Laurel knew he was still there. 'Cristiano?' she asked softly.

'Yes?'

'Thank you.'

Laurel had left her clothes and toiletries in Cristiano's bedroom, and so she stripped off her skirt and slept in her T-shirt and panties. The night was warm, and she opened the windows, breathing in the sultry air. Already the moon was waning, the horizon the pearly grey of early morning. Her body ached and her eyes felt as if they were full of grit. She needed to sleep.

She curled up on the bed, scrunching her eyes tight

and wishing herself back home. Back in her single bed with the patchwork quilt her grandmother had made, the pure, golden light of an Illinois summer streaming through her window. She'd give just about anything to be able to rewind the last three days, go back to the moment where her mother had showed up at her grandfather's farmhouse—Laurel should have closed the door in her face.

Instead she'd let her in. Let her speak. Because stupidly Laurel was always hoping her mother wanted her, not just something from her.

'Darling, you'll never guess,' Elizabeth had announced in a flurry of air kisses and perfume. 'I've met someone.'

Laurel had just stared. This was hardly news.

'He wants to meet you. I want you to meet him.' Elizabeth had smiled mischievously, but Laurel had detected a desperate glitter in her mother's eyes. She was forty-six years old and her days reeling in wealthy businessmen and minor celebrities were surely numbered. 'There might be a ring in my future.'

'Really?' Laurel had said, unsure how she'd felt about that, or anything to do with her mother. She hadn't seen her in two years. Her mother had been in Monaco for her grandfather's funeral three months earlier.

Elizabeth had strode into the living room with its rag rug and faded sofa, and a shudder had gone through her. 'I always hated this place.' She'd looked around, her lip curling. 'Goodness knows why you keep staying.'

'I love it here,' Laurel had said quietly. She placed

one hand on the warm, satiny wood of the newel post. 'It's the only home I've ever known.'

Elizabeth's mouth had tightened. She hated any hint of her deficiencies as a mother. 'I'm sorry I couldn't provide you with a more stable upbringing,' she said stiffly. 'If your father—'

'I didn't mean it like that.'

Elizabeth had turned to look at her directly. 'So will you come to Rome, to meet Rico? It should only take a few days.'

'Rome?' Laurel had boggled at the suggestion. 'Why would I go there? I mean…can't he come here? And why does he have to meet me?'

'Family is important to him. And I need this to work, Laurel.' The desperate look in her mother's eyes had intensified. 'If you do this, I'll give you the only thing you've ever wanted, I promise.' She'd glanced around the worn living room. 'All I'm asking is for you to show Rico that we're a family, that you're pleased to have him in your life. Is that so much to ask?'

Cristiano stretched out on the bed, as far from sleep as he could possibly be, his body still pulsing with the aftershocks of kissing Laurel. Her skin had felt like the supplest silk under his hands. He shifted, trying to suppress the ache in his groin, the flicker of regret whispering through him on dark wings.

He hadn't heard a sound from the bedroom across the hall, not so much as a creak of a floorboard. He hoped Laurel was asleep. She had to be exhausted, after everything she'd endured tonight.

Including him.

Guilt, Cristiano reflected, was a very inconvenient

emotion. It was one he wasn't used to feeling. He'd always prided himself on his plain speaking, his honesty. He never pretended to care. The women he chose to be with knew what he was willing to give, and all that he wasn't, up front. That, in his view, was something admirable. Honourable.

So why did he feel as if his actions tonight hadn't been? As if he'd used Laurel, just as Bavasso had used her? She'd responded to his touch, heaven knew. He'd felt it. He'd certainly felt it in himself, a raging fire he'd struggled to control, the strength of which had alarmed him—because, when he'd taken Laurel in his arms, it had been to prove something to her as well as to himself. Yet he'd had to use all his self-control, all of his deeply ingrained self-discipline, to keep from giving in to the tidal roar of need inside him and drowning in her kiss.

And when Laurel had jerked out of his arms she'd looked...horrified. And hurt. As if he'd damaged her in a way he didn't like to think about.

Restless now, Cristiano rose from his bed and pulled on a T-shirt and drawstring pyjama bottoms. Pale pink morning light seeped along the horizon as the sky lightened to a luminescent grey. He wouldn't sleep. And, he decided as he grabbed his laptop and strode out to the living room, he needed to know more about Laurel Forrester.

Cristiano made himself a mug of strong coffee and then stretched out on one of the sofas, his computer on his lap. He typed her name into the search engine and waited for the results.

He scrolled through pages obviously about other people—a physics professor in Colorado, a housewife in South Carolina—before finally hitting on one that snagged his interest, simply because it was from Illinois. Laurel Forrester, on the page of the website for a hospital in Canton Heights. He frowned, not quite believing this could be his Laurel—because Laurel, whether she acknowledged it or not, was most definitely his. For now, at least.

He clicked and scrolled down the staff directory until he found Laurel Forrester, RN. She was a *nurse*? That so didn't fit the profile of the woman he'd seen totter into La Sirena only a few short hours ago on the arm of one of Rome's shadiest businessmen. Surely that wasn't her?

Cristiano raked a hand through his close-cropped hair, fingernails grazing his skull. He went back to the search results and scrolled through several pages. Then he clicked on images, but not a single one came up that looked like Laurel. Her Internet footprint was light indeed, unlike her mother's.

Just to prove a point to himself, Cristiano typed Elizabeth Forrester's name into the search engine. It didn't take long to find dozens of photos of his former stepmother, usually on the arm of some Z-lister, always looking a little defiant, as if she was daring her audience to ask if she was happy.

Cristiano leaned his head back against the sofa, replaying the moment when he'd seen Laurel come into the casino yesterday evening. He'd been standing by the roulette table, keeping a discreet eye on the heavy betters, making sure nothing got out of hand. His establishments were high class and respectable, where gambling was a dignified pastime rather than a desperate sport.

He'd seen a flash of silver in his peripheral vision, and he'd turned, the nape of his neck prickling, although he hadn't even known why. He'd seen Elizabeth Forrester first, wearing a crimson cocktail dress that was far too tight and short for a woman of her age, although she still had the body to pull it off. His insides had tightened, his mouth turning down in disgust at the sight of the gold-digger who had just about ruined his father's life. And then he'd seen Laurel.

He'd recognised her instantly, even though it had been ten years. It hadn't taken a moment of mental gymnastics, not even a second. He'd looked at her and he'd known. And he'd felt, in that moment, a pang of something deeper than desire—the need to possess, to consume, a craving so overwhelming he struggled to control it.

And then he'd seen whose arm she was on. He'd taken in the skimpy dress and sky-high heels, the bright make-up and hair shellacked with hairspray, and he'd felt as if he could be sick. He *had been* sick, sickened by her obvious tactics, and his stomach had cramped when Bavasso had pulled her onto his lap. She'd perched there, her smile frozen in place, determined to endure…and for what? Had Bavasso paid for the sycophantic attention…and worse? Far worse.

Cristiano had stayed on the fringes of the crowds, watching Laurel and Bavasso out of the corner of his eye, his gut churning. Bavasso went for the baccarat table as he always did, flanked by two of his bodyguards—and Laurel. Elizabeth lurked in the background, looking anxious and trying not to. Clearly this was Laurel's game, but Elizabeth had some stake in it. A mother and daughter team. Had they always been like that? Probably.

He hadn't been able to keep from looking at Laurel, noticing the tiny dress, the slender yet generous figure poured into it. He hadn't thought of Laurel Forrester once in the last ten years, but he realised then that, on some level, it had been a conscious decision. Not thinking of her had taken effort, a matter of will. And he was certainly thinking about her now.

It had taken all his self-control not to stride over to Bavasso when the odious man had pulled Laurel onto his lap. Cristiano had seen the flash of disgust cross Laurel's face but then she'd lifted her chin, her smile firmly in place, and Cristiano hadn't known whether to feel admiration or contempt. She hated this, but she still chose it. That was the kind of woman she was.

So why now was he starting to wonder, even to doubt? He was a man who dealt in certainties. And the certainty he'd seen last night was Laurel agreeing to go up to Bavasso's hotel room. The only reason she'd been in Cristiano's casino with that man was because she'd chosen it. Because she wanted something from him.

Right?

With a sigh Cristiano opened his laptop again and once more he scrolled through the search results for Laurel Forrester. He clicked on the page for the hospital in Illinois again, and went through every page of the website to see if he could find anything more about Laurel Forrester, RN. After half an hour he came across a page of thank you messages and photographs from patients—and there was a photo of Laurel, standing next to an elderly woman and her adult children, looking tired but smiling. He hadn't seen her smile like that all night. It was a genuine smile, full of warmth and kindness, and Cristiano stared and stared at it, unable to look away. Who was the woman in the photo? And who was the woman who had locked herself in his guest bedroom, defiant and afraid?

Cristiano shoved his laptop away. His eyes were gritty, his head starting to pound. Outside sunlight was spreading across the city sky like melted butter, pearly grey giving way to pale, fragile blue. Cristiano opened the sliding glass doors to the private terrace and breathed in the summer air, fresh this early in the morning, yet already imbued with heat.

He curled his hands around the railing as he gazed down at the city starting to wake up, lorries and motorbikes filling the narrow, ancient streets. Laurel would wake up soon too, and then what? They needed to have a conversation, something he hadn't anticipated. He'd expected a simple transaction, and one that was welcome on both sides. That was what he always got, what he demanded. Instead tonight he'd encountered resistance, animosity and doubt—as well as desire. He needed to figure out what was going on, and who Laurel was, before he made his next move.

A sound from the penthouse had him stilling. Over the muted roar of early-morning traffic far below he heard it again, a sound almost like a moan or a cry. Quickly Cristiano strode from the terrace, closing the doors behind him. In the sudden, muted stillness of the penthouse he froze, straining to listen.

There it was again—an anguished moan, coming from Laurel's room. Was she hurt? In pain? Every protective instinct Cristiano had rose to the fore, propelling him across the living room and down the hall.

He knocked sharply on the bedroom door. 'Laurel?'

Silence—and then a whimpering cry. Cristiano tried the handle, rattling it uselessly, as he knew the door was locked. '*Laurel*. Answer me. Are you hurt?'

The only response was a shuddering sob. Cristiano didn't think—he just acted. Backing up a few steps, he rammed the door with his shoulder. It took a few tries, and would create a few bruises, but the lock finally busted and the door sprang open.

With the curtains drawn against the dawn light it took Cristiano's eyes a few desperate seconds to adjust, and then he saw Laurel lying in bed, the sheets twisted around her slender body, her eyes clenched shut, her face an agonised grimace. She was in the throes of a nightmare.

'*Laurel*.' Cristiano spoke gently now as he crept towards the bed and touched her shoulder. 'Laurel, you're dreaming. It's all right. Wake up.'

Laurel's body shuddered with the force of emotion he could see on her face, twisting her features as if she were in agony. 'Don't…' she murmured brokenly. 'Please don't… I don't want to…' Another cry and she pressed her face into the pillow.

It took Cristiano a few shocked seconds to realise, with icy horror, that she was reliving Bavasso's attack. He felt sick—sickened not just by Bavasso, but by himself. His arrogant self-assurance that Laurel would welcome his attention. Hell, that she'd be grateful.

'Laurel.' His voice was soft as he gently touched her shoulder again. 'Laurel, *cara*. Please wake up.' He shook her shoulder, carefully, not wanting to startle or scare her.

And then she did wake up with a sudden gasp, as if she were coming up out of water, as if she'd been drowning. Her face was pale and shocked, her eyes wide and unfocused.

Relief pulsed through him, stronger than anything he'd felt in a long time. 'Laurel, *cara*, you're okay. It was just a dream.'

She blinked a few times, and Cristiano couldn't tell if she had fully come conscious or was still in the hazy throes of her nightmare.

'It wasn't a dream,' she whispered, and she let out a broken little cry. 'It was real.'

'Oh, *cara*.' Cristiano reached for her, not even thinking about what he was doing as he hauled Laurel against his chest, moving onto the bed so she could snuggle against him. The feel of Laurel in his arms— her head burrowing into his chest, her body curled into his—felt supremely right, touching him deeply in a place he'd thought didn't exist. A place he'd excised long ago. 'It's okay,' he whispered. 'You're safe here.' And he knew he meant it.

CHAPTER SIX

THE VESTIGES OF the nightmare clung to her like a grey, snaking mist, obscuring her vision. Obliterating rational thought. Laurel felt Cristiano's arms close around her and they were warm and strong, encasing her in a way that made her feel safe. Protected. *Cherished.*

Some small part of her brain whispered for her to resist this new offensive of his but the nightmare was still too strong—the memory of Bavasso's sneering face, his hands pawing at her—and Cristiano was murmuring to her, his voice steady and low, a humming in her chest. Then he gently shifted her over so he was lying on the bed and she was in his arms, her body close to his, and that felt so very right.

Laurel nestled against him and closed her eyes, not wanting to move. Definitely not wanting to think. The nightmare was still there, lurking, like the monster under the bed, the skeleton in the cupboard. She shuddered and Cristiano's arms tightened around her.

'It's okay,' he whispered. 'You're safe here.'

Even in the grip of her nightmare she knew she shouldn't believe him. She shouldn't trust him. And yet she did, because right now she needed someone to trust. Someone to hold her and tell her she was safe. So she burrowed deeper into the strong wall of Cristiano's chest, closing her eyes and her heart to the memory of his cold, flat statements; to that awful, clinical look on his face in the mirror as he'd touched her body.

Cristiano stroked her back, her hair, whispering soothing words in Italian. It sounded like water rippling over stones, like music. She closed her eyes and tried to make the monster retreat. But Bavasso was still there, lingering on the edges of her mind. It had all happened so *quickly*.

After his assurances that they would all go upstairs for champagne, that this was a family celebration, it had turned into something else in the space of a second. The door to the hotel suite had closed behind her and, before Laurel had so much as been able to blink, he'd been grabbing her, his mouth on hers, his hands on her body. She'd frozen, unable to process what was happening; then, when she'd felt Bavasso squeeze her breast, she'd started to fight, kicking and screaming, nails contacting with flesh. Bavasso had let out an agonised roar, and that had only spurred her on. It had been make or break. Life or death. Eventually she'd made it out through the door, with his hot breath on her neck, his curses renting the air.

'Laurel. *Laurel.*' Cristiano's hands cradled her face and Laurel realised she was weeping, silent tears streaking down her face. She tilted her face up to his as he gently wiped her tears away with his thumbs. It was a gesture so tender and intimate, it made everything in her yearn.

No one had ever touched her like this, yet this was *Cristiano*, a man who had shown her very little understanding or compassion. A man who seemed to think she was little better than a whore. A man whose caress made her feel as if he were touching her with sweet fire, warming and burning her all at once. And suddenly she wanted to be burned.

The distant part in her brain that had been reminding her how stupid this all was, how dangerous, fell silent. Her lips parted. Cristiano's compassionate gaze stilled, fastening on her mouth. The whole room seemed to shimmer.

'Laurel…'

She liked the way he said her name. She liked it far better than *bella*. When he said her name, she felt he knew her. She felt known, and that felt wonderful. Her body arched, just a little, towards his. It was enough.

Cristiano let out a tiny sigh and then he lowered his head, his hands still cradling her face, and brushed his lips against hers. This kiss was entirely different from the calculated and passionate assault in the hallway. This was a balm, a gift—one she accepted, her lips parting under his, her hands coming up to clutch handfuls of his T-shirt. Cristiano's breath came out in a shudder and the kiss deepened, turning both hungry and yet still so achingly sweet. She wanted to be kissed like this for ever—and yet already she wanted more.

Cristiano's breathing was harsh and ragged as he shifted on the bed, pulling her closer to him so their legs twined together and their hips nudged, the press of his arousal against her stomach electrifying. Pulses of desire were zinging through her, short-circuiting her thoughts. Gone were reservations, regrets, resistance. She slid her hands under his shirt, felt the taut muscles and satiny skin of his abs, and let out a shuddering sigh. Cristiano drew his breath in sharply as she let her hands drift across his chest, revelling in the hot, hard feel of him.

'Laurel…' This time her name was a warning. She didn't like that quite as much.

'Please,' she whispered, her eyes fluttering closed. 'Please touch me.'

She wanted to be touched. She needed to feel desired and treasured and loved, just for a little while. She knew it wasn't real; of course she did. She wasn't that naïve, that *stupid*. But just for a few hours, a few moments, even, she wanted this. Him. She wanted pleasure and closeness and touch. And she didn't want to think about the consequences.

'You make me feel beautiful,' she whispered as his lips moved over her skin, from her jaw to her throat. Her hands bunched on his arms, her palms rounding over his taut biceps. 'You make me feel desired.'

'You are desired,' Cristiano said, his voice a husky growl, his lips brushing her heated, over-sensitised skin. 'I promise you that.'

Laurel let out another shuddering sigh as Cristiano's mouth moved lower. He slipped his hands under the silky T-shirt she'd slept in, and when his palms cupped her breasts she moaned out loud. How could this feel so impossibly good? So wonderfully right? But it did. It did… And yet the aching restlessness surging through her body and settling between her thighs made her realise even this wasn't enough.

She wanted it all.

Cristiano slid her T-shirt higher and then his mouth was on her, teasing, tormenting, touching her in a way she'd never been touched before. Laurel arced off the bed, her hands clutching his head, anchoring him to her. Still needing more.

'Cristiano…' She gasped out his name and his head moved lower, his tongue teasing her navel, then moving even lower, lips brushing the tender skin of her belly. He was going to touch her—kiss her—*there*. It seemed like the most intimate, sacred act. The most revealing and vulnerable. Laurel's whole body tensed as taut as a bow, waiting, straining…

And then Cristiano hesitated, his lips pressed to her stomach, just below her belly button. 'Are you sure about this…?' he began, and Laurel let out a ragged laugh.

'*Yes.*'

'You've just been through an ordeal…'

Now he mentioned that? Now he showed compassion and understanding? 'Don't you dare develop a conscience now,' she said, her voice coming out in ragged pants. 'Don't you *dare.*'

He laughed softly. 'Very well. I won't.' And then his mouth moved lower, his tongue knowing exactly what to do, how to send lightning streaks of pleasure ripping jaggedly through her, and Laurel let out a sound she'd never made before—half-scream, half-sob. Her body felt as if it were splintering into crystalline fragments, a rainbow of sensation arcing through her. She let out another shattering sob, and then Cristiano was on top of her, a heavy yet comforting and necessary weight that she welcomed utterly, and then, yes— finally, amazingly—he was sliding inside her, the sensation both so unexpected and wonderfully right.

She felt a twinge of pain, a chafing sensation as he

moved within her, and Cristiano paused. Cursed. That, Laurel suspected hazily, wasn't supposed to happen.

'You can't be…' he breathed, his body poised over hers, the muscles in his arms corded, a sheen of sweat on his brow.

She tilted her face up to his, her body pulsing with need, pulsing around him. A strong, sweet craving made her arch her hips as she tried to draw him deeper into herself, searching for an elusive something she couldn't even articulate but knew she needed. 'I can't be what?'

Cristiano's face was contorted, his teeth gritted with the effort of holding back. *'Vergine,'* he bit out. 'Tell me you're not.'

She didn't know much Italian, but that word was pretty self-explanatory. For a second Laurel thought about lying. Cristiano hardly seemed like a man with many arrows on his moral compass, but perhaps this was one of them: deflowering virgins. Yet, when it came down to it, she didn't think she could lie. And in any case she didn't think such a lie would be believable. Her body told its own truth.

'Does it matter?' Laurel asked softly, because to her it didn't. She'd needed this. Asked for it. Demanded it, even. So why was Cristiano looking so anguished? This had been her choice, not his. 'Remember what I said about that conscience?' she gasped out.

'I remember.' His expression had turned grim, and Laurel faltered. He was *inside* her, for heaven's sake. Was he really going to stop now? It was a little late for regrets.

'Cristiano…' She put her arms around his shoulders, smoothing her palms down his back, drawing him closer to her. Gasping as, his jaw still clenched, he slid deeper inside, filling her up. And then, with a groan, he started to move.

And the slightly strange sensation of being filled up exploded into something else entirely. Something huge and wonderful and soul-changing as Laurel started to match his rhythm and then began to fragment all over again.

A virgin. He never would have guessed. Certainly hadn't expected it. With his body still pulsing with the aftershocks of the most explosive orgasm he'd ever had, Cristiano rolled onto his back and stared at the ceiling. Tried to untangle the churn of what he felt— guilt, pleasure, anger and a deep, primal pride because he'd been her first. Her only.

He gave up the task because the feelings were too tightly twined to separate. And he needed to figure out what to do now.

He glanced at Laurel, who was also staring at the ceiling, a pensive look on her face. Her body was flushed and rosy, her lips swollen, her hair spread on the pillow in a glorious, golden swirl. Looking at her made him want her all over again, even as the sweat dried on his skin and his heart still thudded.

A *virgin.* What was he supposed to do with that?

'Well.' She let out a soft, satisfied little sigh that, impossibly, made him smile. 'I'm glad I experienced that.'

As if he were a tourist attraction, a Ferris wheel or a rather interesting museum. He didn't know whether to be annoyed or flattered. She turned to him, her eyebrows raised, a small and endearingly uncertain smile on her face. 'Are you?'

Was he? Most definitely. Sex with Laurel Forrester had been…mind-blowing. The best sex he'd ever had, and he'd had a lot. But she'd been a *virgin*. And he shouldn't have taken advantage. She'd been having a nightmare, remembering an attack only hours earlier. And he'd just stolen her innocence.

Laurel might doubt it, but Cristiano had a code of honour and his behaviour just now—hell, his behaviour since Laurel had stumbled into his flat—violated it. That was not something he could accept.

And, as for how she'd made him feel, the places she'd reached inside him, well, that was something he could not even begin to think about.

'It's taking you a while to answer, so I'm guessing not.' Laurel's voice wobbled a little and she sat up, reaching for the T-shirt Cristiano had tossed over her head at some point. He couldn't even remember when. The last hour felt like a golden blur of exquisite feeling. He hadn't been in control of anything, and that was something else he couldn't accept.

This wasn't who he was—someone controlled by desire, motivated by lust. Unable to keep from wanting a woman. Just like his father.

'I did enjoy it,' he said, his voice coming out flat. 'Obviously. But you should have told me you were a virgin earlier.'

Laurel shrugged the T-shirt on and then turned to him, one golden-brown eyebrow raised. 'And you would have believed me?'

No, he wouldn't have. Not in a million years. 'Still,' Cristiano said, because he couldn't think of anything better and, damn it, she *should* have told him. He should have known.

'I think it's my decision whether I release that information or not,' Laurel said a little coolly. 'Not yours. It's my body, after all.'

'But I have a responsibility—'

'No, I have a responsibility.' Laurel cut him off. 'To myself. And I chose to have sex with you so, guess what, Cristiano, you're off the hook. Although why you've put yourself on the hook, I have no idea. You didn't seem to be so consumed by morals earlier in the evening when you were suggesting one of your *arrangements*.'

He deserved that, but it still chafed. 'This is completely different.'

'Is it? Why? Because I'm not who you thought I was?'

He thought of the photo of her with those patients. No, she wasn't who he thought she was. At least, it seemed she was more than that. 'Why were you with Bavasso tonight?' he demanded. 'Why were you acting like…like his trollop?' The words burst out of him unfairly, but he was jealous. And angry.

Hurt flashed across her face, then her expression shuttered and she looked away. 'I don't want to talk about that.'

'I do.'

'Too bad.'

'Damn it, Laurel,' he snapped, his temper starting to fray. 'I deserve to know.'

'Why? Just because you slept with me?' She lifted her chin, eyes flashing. 'I doubt you demand such rights of the legion of women you've slept with.'

'You don't know anything about me.'

'And you don't know anything about me,' she answered, rising from the bed. She tugged the T-shirt down in a useless attempt to cover her bottom. 'So we're even. Now, if you don't mind, I'd like you to go.'

'I do mind.' He settled against the bed, arms folded. He still didn't know exactly what he wanted from this situation, but it definitely wasn't to be kicked to the kerb. He was the one who decided when things ended. *If* they ended.

Laurel stared him down, her lower lip pushed out, her eyes narrowed. 'What do you want from me?' she demanded in a low voice.

Hell if he knew. 'Why are you a virgin?'

'Why?' She stared at him incredulously. 'Why do you care?'

'Humour me.'

She shook her head slowly. 'There's no pleasing you, is there? You branded me a whore and, now you know I'm a virgin, you so obviously aren't happy with that either.'

He didn't need his unreasonableness pointed out to him. 'Why?' he gritted.

'Why not? Is there a law that says twenty-four-year-olds can't be virgins?'

'Practically. Most women…'

'I am not most women.'

She was an utter enigma, and he didn't like that. He needed things to be straightforward. Women to be what they seemed. He needed Laurel to be what she'd seemed, what he'd assumed, because the alternative made his stomach cramp with acidic regret for the way he'd behaved. The things he'd said—and done.

She drew herself up, all haughty dignity, and then ruined the effect by tugging again on her T-shirt. Her legs looked endless and golden, and he couldn't keep from remembering how silky her skin had felt.

'So you're just going to stay here?' she asked in a chilly voice. 'In my bed?'

'My bed, actually.'

She pressed her lips together, looking suddenly far more vulnerable than proud, and Cristiano wished he hadn't tried to score such a petty point. He was above such tactics, surely? And yet… Laurel had unsettled him so much. He felt completely wrong-footed. Wrong everything.

He glanced out at the sky, now the palest of blues. It was a little past seven in the morning after the longest night of his life. 'Perhaps you should get some more sleep,' he said, rising from the bed in one fluid movement, then reaching for his drawstring bottoms. 'We can talk later.'

Laurel folded her arms, a movement meant to make her look strong, but she looked as if she was holding herself together. Literally. 'About what?'

'Everything,' Cristiano said, then he strode from the room.

CHAPTER SEVEN

LAUREL LISTENED TO the door slam shut behind Cristiano and let out a weary breath. That had been exhausting. Her body was still tingling with the memory of his touch, her heart thudding from the sharp words they'd just exchanged. She'd acted far more assured and confident than she really felt. The truth was she felt like a quivering bowlful of jelly inside.

She'd known sex with Cristiano would rock her world. Burn her up. And here she was, feeling utterly singed.

With a shudder, Laurel sat on the bed, drawing her knees up to her chest. The last she'd wanted after her first experience of sex was an interrogation about what she'd been doing with Bavasso and why she'd been a virgin.

Cristiano had almost seemed angry, and so unmoved by what they'd just done. Yet how could that surprise her? The legion of women he'd had…his face in the mirror. No, the only surprise was how stupid she was. Again. And yet even now she couldn't regret it.

The feel of his hands on her…his body inside her… Laurel shuddered again, this time with longing. She'd never felt anything so intimate or intense or…incredible before. It felt far more *important* than she'd expected. Of course, it wasn't important to Cristiano. It definitely didn't mean anything. She knew that, yet… she couldn't keep from feeling changed, as if something inside her had shifted for ever. She would have a tie to Cristiano now, no matter what happened in the future. An unbreakable tie, at least for her, even if he forgot her name in a few weeks.

Beyond all that, experiencing such pleasure made her want to know it again. To feel Cristiano's hands on her, his body…

Yet she knew she wouldn't. For her own health and sanity. And in any case she doubted Cristiano would ask. He'd got what he wanted. She was undoubtedly out of his system now, and he would be on to the next woman, another conquest. She'd fallen so easily.

With a sigh Laurel curled up on the bed, fatigue crashing over her. She'd barely slept all night, her one attempt tormented by nightmares. She'd sleep now, if she could, and then she'd deal with Cristiano. No matter what had happened between them, she needed to find a way forward. A way back home.

When Laurel awoke bright, lemony sunlight was spilling through the windows and the room was warm. It was midday, and she'd been asleep for hours. Feeling muddle-headed, Laurel took another shower, and when she came out she saw Cristiano had moved all the clothes to this bedroom. They lay on the end of her freshly made bed in neat piles, making her feel vaguely uneasy. If he was sending a message, she didn't know what it was.

She dressed in a simple sheath dress of lavender linen, which felt too fancy, but there wasn't anything more casual. Then she put her damp hair up in a twist, took a deep breath and headed out.

Cristiano wasn't in the living area as she expected, and she wandered through the sprawling space before she found him in a glassed-in alcove on the far side, clearly a study area. He was seated at a desk, his laptop open in front of him, wearing a black button-down shirt and charcoal-grey trousers. He turned as she approached, and Laurel had to suppress a stab of desire at the sight of him freshly showered and shaven, his hair still damp, his silvery eyes as piercing as twin blades.

'Good morning.'

'Good afternoon, actually,' she returned with an attempt at a laugh. 'I didn't expect to sleep so long.'

'I'm glad you did.' He turned back to his laptop, pressed a few buttons and then shut it with a decisive snap. 'So.' He swivelled back to face her, his gaze coolly appraising.

'So.' Laurel took a deep breath and buoyed her courage. 'I think I can brave Bavasso.' She kept her voice light but firm. 'I'll risk it, anyway. I want—I need—to go home.' Her voice wobbled a little at the last, but she kept her gaze steady on Cristiano's inscrutable face. Why did he have to be so beautiful? He was all sharp angles and clear, hard lines, the purity of his silver eyes a perfect foil to his olive skin and inky dark hair. It made it hard to keep his gaze. Hard too to keep her nerve.

'Where is home, incidentally?' He'd reverted to that mild voice that hid so much. Made her wary.

'I told you, a small town in Illinois.'

'Canton Heights?'

So he'd done an Internet search on her. 'Yes.'

Something flickered across his face like a ripple in water and then was gone. 'You work as a nurse.'

'You've done some homework.' She lifted her chin. 'Yes. Does it matter?'

'Not particularly.' Now she heard disinterest, and for some stupid reason it stung. 'But you can't go home just yet.'

'I think you're overreacting about Bavasso.'

Cristiano arched an eyebrow. 'And how could you possibly make such a judgement?'

'It's just…' She couldn't make such a judgement, but she had to try. Had to get out of here, for her own sake, and she didn't have any other options besides the obvious one: leave. 'He'll get over it, surely? He barely knew me. And he cares about my mother…' she trailed off, afraid that wasn't true.

'Cares about your mother? Where on earth did you get that idea?'

Of course, Laurel would rather her mother broke things off with Bavasso, but she questioned whether she would, even now.

'He attacked you last night, Laurel, and he would have done far worse if you hadn't escaped. Surely you haven't forgotten that already?'

Anger leaped inside her at his admonishing tone. 'Of course not.'

'Or the ensuing nightmare you had?'

Memory shimmered in the air between them, memory of her nightmare and also how he had comforted her. Laurel looked away, hating herself for being so affected by him. 'Of course I remember everything, Cristiano. It was only a couple of hours ago. But surely it's my decision, not yours, about whether I risk Rico Bavasso's fury?' She hadn't meant to make it a question.

'As I have said before, it is not. Not when you have no idea what you're asking.'

'Stop treating me like a child,' Laurel snapped, and Cristiano's eyes flashed like a glint of light on metal.

'I am not treating you like a child,' he said in a low, lethal voice that slid inside her like a cold blade. 'I am treating you as someone who is out of her depth and experience, which you cannot deny. I don't know how or why you got involved with someone like Bavasso, Laurel, but trust me, you are in over your head.'

More than he knew. She was in over her head not just with Rico Bavasso but with the man in front of her. Cristiano Ferrero felt far more dangerous to her now than the sleek silver fox staying several floors below. She could hardly say that now, however.

'So what are you suggesting? That you keep me captive in your penthouse until Bavasso moves on?'

'That would hardly accomplish our purpose.'

'Which is?'

'To show Bavasso that you are mine.' Cristiano spoke coolly but heat flared in his eyes, turning them nearly to gold. *His.* She'd been his only hours ago, marked for ever by every touch of his hand, every brush of his lips. Laurel fought not to blush.

'And how are you going to show that?'

'By appearing with you tonight, as I mentioned before. Perhaps you have forgotten?'

Last night was a blur of panic and disbelief. She recalled him saying something along those lines, but she hadn't taken him seriously. Had she? Now she did. Now, judging by the feeling of icy dread seeping into her stomach, she took him very seriously indeed.

'Tonight? That's it?'

'We'll see how it unfolds.'

'So tomorrow I could go home?' she pressed, eager for a deadline. A finish line.

'Not quite.' He paused, his mouth compressing, his silvery gaze flicking over her in cool assessment. 'I believe your stay here will be for two weeks, perhaps a little longer. That should be sufficient.'

'Two *weeks*?' Laurel goggled at him. 'But you said Bavasso would be satisfied in a day or two.'

'It's not Bavasso I'm thinking of.' Cristiano dismissed the man who had loomed like such a threat with the snap of his fingers. 'After our appearance tonight, he will no longer be welcome in any of my establishments. I do not harbour criminals.'

Laurel gulped. 'Okay. Then why two weeks?' She'd only taken a week off work. Laurel swallowed. 'I can't hang around here for two weeks. I have work…'

'I'm sure they'll understand.'

'They're depending on me.'

'Even so.' Cristiano's tone and expression were both implacable. Laurel knew nothing she said would have any effect at all. He was utterly immoveable, untouchable, yet mere hours ago she'd been writhing underneath him, arms and legs wrapped around him, as close to him as she'd been to anyone, ever. She had to stop thinking about that.

'I still don't understand why you want me to stay here for so long.' For his own pleasure? The possibility brought a swift intake of breath, a stupid rush of pleasure, a flash of alarm. Surely not…?

'Don't you?'

'Stop playing games, Cristiano.' Laurel started to get annoyed. 'You can't keep me a prisoner for your own—your own pleasure.'

'That's not why I want you here.'

Ouch. Laurel willed herself not to flush with the humiliation of that flatly spoken assurance. 'You still haven't told me why.'

'I want you here because in approximately four-teen days I'll know whether or not you are carrying my child.'

Cristiano watched with dispassion as shock drained the colour from Laurel's face, turning her eyes into huge, aquamarine pools. Innocent as she was—or rather, had been—she hadn't thought about birth control.

'Judging from your expression,' he said dryly, 'I can assume you are not on the pill?'

'No.'

'Or have taken any other precautionary measures in terms of birth control?'

'No,' Laurel snapped. 'Why should I? I was a *virgin*, in case you've forgotten.'

'I assure you, I have not.'

She took a quick, sharp breath. 'It is very unlikely I'm pregnant.'

'Is it?' Cristiano's calm tone belied the churn of anger, regret and anxiety he felt inside. 'Do you have information of which I am not aware?'

'I don't think I was in that part of my monthly cycle.' Her eyebrows rose in challenge. 'You are knowledgeable of such basic biology?'

'I believe I am.'

'Then you know that the only way I could be pregnant now is if I was ovulating in the last twenty-four hours.'

'And that is a possibility, is it not? You are fertile, I assume? No problems there?'

Her cheeks went pink. 'Not that I know of.'

He spread his hands. 'So we wait.'

She stared at him. 'Two whole weeks?'

'You're the nurse, Laurel. Isn't that how long it takes to get a positive result?'

'Around that, yes, from ovulation.' She spoke reluctantly. 'But I really don't think this is an issue, Cristiano.'

'We'll find out soon enough, won't we?'

'You speak so knowledgeably about all of this.' Laurel's lip curled. 'You have some experience in these matters, I suppose?'

'Actually, no. None of the women I have ever been with has become pregnant.' He'd always taken precautions. Laurel was the only woman with whom he'd lost control—and he had no intention of telling her that. He had no intention of it happening again, either.

'Never?' She looked sceptical and for some reason it annoyed him.

'No, never.' One woman had faked a pregnancy, and Cristiano had insisted she perform a test in his presence. Unpleasant but necessary, and the matter had been resolved quickly. He was not a man to be duped. Not the way his father had been.

'So we wait two weeks. And then what?'

'What happens next depends on whether you are carrying my child.'

The words fell into the stillness, rippled like stones

cast in a pool. Laurel stared at him, her eyes hard and shiny, like glass. 'I'm not pregnant.'

'You don't know that.'

'But if I am,' she continued swiftly, '*I* will decide what to do about my baby.'

Anger fired through him, a clean, burning sweep. He rose from his chair, the movement controlled and precise. 'This child, should it exist, belongs to me as much as it does to you. *We* will decide, *bella*, make no mistake.'

Her jaw tightened, her eyes sparking at him. Cristiano's fists clenched. It was entirely inappropriate that he was turned on at this moment, yet he felt it all the same. Desire, hot and strong, coursed through him, making him want, even now, to take her in his arms and kiss her useless protests away. He took a quick, controlled breath. Now was not the time to indulge in such feelings. He'd already decided he wouldn't touch Laurel Forrester again. She was too tempting. Too dangerous…to his shame.

'You really are a control freak, aren't you?' she said in a low voice that vibrated with fury. 'A heartless one. You'd insist on making the decision about whether I could keep my own child.'

'What?' He stared at her in disbelief. 'What is that supposed to mean?'

Confusion flashed and she bit her lip. 'I assumed you'd want me to have an abortion.'

He felt a deep surge of an emotion he couldn't identify—and then he realised it was hurt, and he hated that he felt it. That he'd let a woman, a woman he barely knew, make him feel it. 'I would never do that,' he said in a low voice. '*Never*. If I really wanted you to get an abortion, I would procure a morning after pill right now.' He'd thought of it, but with the amount of time it would take to get one it seemed risky, and the idea of it repelled him. 'If you are pregnant, I would want you to keep the child. My child.' His throat worked and his chest felt tight. 'Our child.'

'Okay.' She looked surprised, even a little winded, by his vehemence. And he was surprised too. He'd never wanted children. Had never anticipated getting married or having a family. Having those ties that bound and choked. And yet…if, by the hand of Providence, Laurel was pregnant with his baby, there was no question what he would do. He would marry her.

Not that he intended to tell her that now. She looked shell-shocked as it was.

'So…' Laurel licked her lips. 'What would happen, then? If…?'

'We'll discuss that if and when it occurs,' Cristiano answered swiftly. Laurel was still looking flummoxed.

'And for the next two weeks…?'

'You stay with me.'

She cocked her head, a question in her eyes that he knew she didn't dare ask. And he decided to leave the question as to what the nature of their relationship would be unspoken and unanswered. He'd made a decision not to sleep with her, yes, but he wasn't about to reveal that information. He wasn't at all sure if he'd stick to that decision.

Cristiano reached for his mobile phone and thumbed a few buttons. 'I will arrange for the necessary wardrobe, cosmetics and stylists.'

Laurel's mouth dropped open. 'What?'

'You have no clothes.'

'You just got me some clothes, and I have more back at my hotel—'

'Appropriate clothes,' Cristiano amended. 'As my... companion, you need to be dressed and styled in a certain way.'

Laurel's mouth pursed. 'Like a doll, you mean.'

'No, like an elegant, beautiful, accomplished woman. The only kind I have on my arm.'

She laughed at that, a hard note to the sound. 'So those supermodels are accomplished?'

'In their own way.' Admittedly, intelligence or wit had not been high on his list of desirable qualities for a sexual liaison. 'I can hardly have you traipsing about in a dress like the one you wore last night,' he added.

She flinched and looked away. 'You seem to like reminding me of that.'

'"Like" is not the word I'd use.'

'Isn't it?' She swung back to challenge him with a glare. Heat flared deep inside again. He didn't usually like to be questioned or challenged, but something about Laurel's attempts to stand her ground, the innocent bravery of it, made him admire her as well as want her. Both emotions were inconvenient at the moment.

'I accept that you were playing a part,' he said levelly. 'Or something like that. And I will find out why soon enough.'

'Will you?' she scoffed.

'Yes,' Cristiano said, and his voice vibrated with the force of his feeling. No matter what the next two weeks held, he fully intended to get to the bottom of the enigma that was Laurel Forrester. 'I will.'

CHAPTER EIGHT

CRISTIANO WAS AS good as his word. Within an hour of the calls he'd placed, people started arriving—women dressed all in black, with heels higher than the ones Laurel had worn last night, carrying expensive-looking garment bags, glimpses of silk and satin visible on the padded hangers.

A team of white-coated beauticians came in as well, wheeling in cases and equipment and making Laurel blink. She'd never had so much as a manicure in her entire life, and it looked as if they were setting up an entire beauty salon in her bedroom.

She glanced at Cristiano; his expression was impassive, almost bored, as he watched the parade of experts march in. But when he caught her eye he gave her the tiniest glimmer of a smile which, inexplicably, made her heart lift.

'I know you're about to tell me how ridiculous this all is,' he said in a low, lazy voice. 'But why don't you enjoy being pampered for a bit?'

There were a lot of reasons why she shouldn't enjoy anything about this. He was making her over because she wasn't good enough. She didn't even want to be here. And as for the chance that she was pregnant...

Well. There was nothing she could do about any of it. One of the army of women pressed a glass into her hand and, bemused, Laurel glanced down at the green drink.

'What…?'

'Spinach, kale, almond and banana smoothie,' the woman said. 'With flax seeds and Omega 3 oils. Does wonders for your skin.'

And actually tasted surprisingly delicious. Over the rim of her glass Laurel caught Cristiano's eye again. This time he was smiling properly, and it made her realise she hadn't actually seen him smile—a real smile, not that cold curving of his lips—since she'd first stumbled into his penthouse.

'I'll leave you to it,' he said softly, and disappeared in the direction of his study while Laurel let herself be ushered back into her bedroom.

The next few hours were a whirl of treatments as beauticians slathered every inch of her body with some unguent, oil or scrub, and others worked on her fingers and toes, filing, buffing and polishing. A woman gave her a head massage while some kind of seaweed mask dried on her face and Laurel decided that this was a rabbit hole she would happily disappear down for a while. She'd never felt so pampered or relaxed, and she forced herself not to think about all the 'what if?'s that still loomed, or what the next two weeks were going to look like.

She'd called the hospital, and with they'd been relaxed about her taking the time off, given all the vacation time she had saved up. So maybe, just maybe, she could enjoy *some* of this enforced holiday.

After her hair, face and body had all been dealt with

she was swathed in an enormous robe of the softest terry cloth and shown gown after gown after gown. Not that she was actually given a say. One of the assistants whisked a gown away before she'd even had a chance to touch the satiny material.

'Wrong colour,' the woman said briskly, thrusting the dress back in the wardrobe.

Laurel ended up trying on several evening gowns, all haute couture, incredibly well made and even more expensive.

'This one for tonight,' one of the women declared when Laurel tried on an emerald-green gown with a diamanté halter top. The stylist was tall and thin, dressed all in black, her dark hair pulled back into a bun so tight her eyes were nearly watering.

'Tonight…?' Laurel stared at her blankly even as those *what ifs* started creeping into her consciousness, dread curdling her stomach.

'Yes, tonight.' The woman pursed her lips. 'Signor Ferrero was very specific about what he wanted.'

'Was he?' The enjoyment Laurel had been feeling at being pampered, the relaxation that had seeped like honey into her very bones, drained away. 'What did he want?'

The assistant didn't hear, or pretended not to hear. 'Now your make-up and hair,' she said, and led Laurel to a chair, where a band of women armed with hairdryers and straighteners was waiting.

An hour later Laurel was ready—although, for what, she didn't even know. Her hair had been straightened and then pulled back into an elegant chignon. Diamond teardrop earrings dangled from each ear, and as for her face…

When she finally got to examine her reflection, Laurel was amazed and more than a little disconcerted. She looked like a stranger. A very elegant, glamorous and, yes, even beautiful stranger. Discreet eye shadow and mascara made her eyes look huge. Bronzer and contouring made her cheekbones stand out like blades. Crimson lipstick made her mouth look plump, full and blood-red. She didn't know whether to be pleased or horrified by what she saw. In any case, she just felt numb.

'Signor Ferrero is waiting,' the woman with the tight bun announced and, with her fingernails digging into Laurel's elbow, she led her out of the bedroom and back into the living area of the penthouse.

Twilight was stealing over the city, lights beginning to twinkle far below, the sky the pale violet of a bruise. Laurel minced her way across the slick marble floor; the silver-heeled stilettos she wore were even higher than the ones she'd had on last night, and the dress puddled around her ankles, making her feel as if she were in some sort of elegant strait jacket.

'Signor Ferrero is on the terrace,' the woman murmured, then headed back to the bedroom. Laurel could hear the other assistants starting to pack up all their equipment. She took a deep breath and carefully made her way across the floor to the open doors on the far side of the living room. She hadn't even realised the penthouse had a terrace, but now she could see Cristiano standing on a wide balcony framed with potted plants, gazing out at the city.

She paused on the threshold, the balmy summer breeze blowing over her. Her heart was stuttering in her chest for all sorts of reasons. She had no idea what was going to happen tonight. What she would be expected to do. And as for Cristiano...

He looked magnificent in a tuxedo, the jacket encasing his broad shoulders to perfection, the crisp snowy whiteness of his shirt the perfect foil to his dark hair and olive skin.

Then he turned and Laurel caught her breath, because the heat flaring in Cristiano's eyes made her remember last night in all its exquisite detail. She didn't want the reminder, didn't need it, to complicate what already felt fraught. With what felt like superhuman effort she banished the memory and stepped out onto the terrace.

'So here I am, all dolled up with nowhere to go.'

His eyes simmered like liquid silver, his mouth a compressed line. Laurel had the sudden urge to run her hand along his chiselled jaw with its hint of sexy stubble. To feel his skin under her fingers again. 'On the contrary. You have somewhere to go.'

Her heart stuttered in her chest. 'Where?'

'Down to the casino. With me.'

Laurel swallowed dryly. The last time she'd been on that casino floor... 'Tonight? I mean, so soon? If I'm going to be here for two weeks...' She trailed off, a desperate note entering her voice. She didn't want to go down there. Didn't want to see Bavasso again, or be another ornament on someone's arm, even Cristiano's. Especially Cristiano's.

'Of course so soon,' Cristiano answered in a clipped voice. 'Why wait? The sooner Bavasso realises you're mine, the better.'

'Maybe I don't want to be anyone's.'

'Too late, *bella*, and too bad. You don't have a

choice any more.' Cristiano's smile was hard, the kind of smile she was used to, the kind she really didn't like. 'You should have thought of that before you tangled with Bavasso. Fortunately, I think this can be resolved quickly. The sooner Bavasso is off my property, the better.'

'Fine, let's go,' Laurel said, and held out her hand.

Mistake. Cristiano's palm slid across her, jolting her senses. Reminding her of…everything. Lips, tongues, hands, legs, bodies. Skin…smooth and hot and hard. *Stroking…*

She really had to stop thinking like this.

Cristiano's fingers tightened on hers, reminding her that she was under his control. She was his…at least for the next two weeks. And in spite of everything, against all sense and odds, Laurel felt a lick of excitement through her veins. Anticipation fizzed in her stomach and she decided not to suppress it for once. She needed the hit to make it through this evening.

They rode in silence down the lift, its speed making Laurel feel dizzy. Or perhaps Cristiano was the one making her feel dizzy, with her hand still in his, the spicy scent of his aftershave, the heat of his body, the overwhelming maleness of him, dominating her senses. She couldn't think, could barely breathe.

'So what happens when we go into the casino?' she asked, her voice breathy with nerves.

'Follow my lead.' Cristiano's voice was grim. 'And, for the love of heaven, do a better job of playing a mistress with me than you did with Bavasso.' He glanced at her, eyes and teeth both glinting. 'That shouldn't be too hard, since you *are* my mistress.'

The doors opened before Laurel could make a stinging comeback and, with his careless remark still thudding through her, she followed him out onto the crowded casino floor.

Nothing about this felt as he'd anticipated. Needed. Laurel was stunning, but she wasn't Laurel. When she'd appeared on the terrace, Cristiano had fought the nonsensical urge to take the pins from her hair, to grab his handkerchief and wipe the crimson lipstick from her luscious mouth. To strip her of her dress and heels and put her back in the plain T-shirt and skirt she'd worn earlier, or preferably nothing at all. He didn't want her like this, looking like all his other mistresses, glamorous, edgy and hard.

But that was exactly how he'd wanted her to look. Exactly what he'd told the army of assistants to make her look like, because she needed to look like his mistress. She was his mistress...of a sort.

Not liking it didn't make sense. It made him feel angry and strangely vulnerable, two emotions he despised. So he wouldn't feel them. Cristiano paused on the threshold of the casino as a cold, steely calm came over him. He was here to show Bavasso that Laurel was his, for Laurel's sake as well as his own. The reputation of his hotel and casino, of his professional status, rested on keeping men like Bavasso in check, or preferably off the premises. The sooner this irritation was dealt with, the better.

Bavasso was certainly unpleasant, but Cristiano wasn't really worried about him. And he might have overplayed Bavasso's reputation in order to secure his own interest in Laurel. He felt a qualm of guilt about that and shoved it away. He'd deal with Bavasso tonight and tomorrow, and the next two weeks, would be his and Laurel's.

Raising his chin, Cristiano coldly scanned the room with its baccarat and blackjack, poker tables and roulette wheel. Diamonds glinted and the buzz of conversation, glasses clinking and dice being rolled, filled the room.

Cristiano had never gambled. He hated the thought of it, the desperate need for the adrenalin rush, the loss of control, the craven craving. Casinos were a necessary part of a luxury hotel chain, but he'd never placed money on a bet. Never held his breath for the roll of the dice. It wasn't the kind of man he was.

So why did bringing Laurel onto this heaving floor feel like a risk?

Next to him she shifted nervously, and he caught the scent of her perfume, something unfamiliar and cloyingly expensive, not the scent of lemon and violets he'd smelled earlier.

'What exactly am I meant to be doing?' she whispered. The pulse leapt in her throat as her gaze darted around the crowded room.

'All you have to do is look beautiful and smile,' Cristiano said. 'I think you can manage that.' He glanced at her, his mouth curving in what he intended to be a reassuring smile, but she didn't look as if he'd put her at ease at all.

Her face was pale, her eyes wide, her slender hands clenched into fists at her sides. 'Relax,' Cristiano murmured. 'We have to be convincing.'

'Why?'

'Because I would like to deal with Bavasso and be

done with him. If he suspects he's being played, he'll continue to annoy the both of us.'

'You make him sound like a fly.'

'And I will swat him away.' Cristiano reached for her hand. Her palm was icy cold in his as he pulled her deeper into the room and the throng of curious on-lookers. He was used to being looked at, the owner of La Sirena and notorious in his own right. Women eyed Laurel up and down, mouths twisting in disappoint-ment or derision. Men eyed her lasciviously, making everything in Cristiano tighten. She was his, damn it. *His.* He didn't even want them looking.

This was starting to feel like a very bad idea.

He pulled Laurel along, deeper into the crowd. She stumbled slightly, muttering under her breath, almost making Cristiano smile. She disliked the dressing up almost as much as he did.

'Now what?' she whispered.

'Enjoy.' He slid his arm around her waist, splay-ing his fingers along her hip. He felt her react, and it afforded him a flare of primal pleasure. Yes, she was his, whether she acknowledged it or not. Whether she wanted to be or not. They had a connection, a bond, forged in desire. She couldn't break it, and he didn't want to. Yet.

Laurel's body was tense under his arm as he moved her towards his usual place by the roulette table. Ba-vasso hadn't come in yet, although Cristiano expected him. He'd heard from his staff that he was still in Rome, and when he was he came to La Sirena nearly every night.

Idly Cristiano stroked Laurel's hip and her body twanged in response. 'You look like you're at the dentist,' he murmured, leaning closer so his breath fanned her ear. She shivered. 'I told you, relax.'

'I can't.'

'You're safe here, Laurel. I won't let anyone hurt you.' That was a promise he was absolutely sure he'd keep.

She just shook her head a fraction, her expression as pained as if she were having a filling done. Annoyance sparked inside him.

'You were a better actress with Bavasso,' he growled, further annoyed that he felt irritated and, yes, even a little hurt by how difficult she was finding this. *Him*.

'That was different.'

'How?'

Her tongue darted out to lick crimson lips. 'It just was.'

'Maybe you need a drink.' He snapped his fingers and a waiter came scurrying. 'Champagne,' Cristiano ordered. 'And two glasses.'

'Very good, sir.'

His narrowed gaze continued to survey the room as he stroked Laurel's hip, willing her to soften. 'Is it so very difficult,' he murmured, 'for you to appear as if you enjoy my company? Because you enjoyed it last night.'

'I wonder,' she breathed, 'how long you're going to keep reminding me of that.'

'As long as it takes for you to begin to relax.'

'Reminding me of my complete and utter folly is hardly going to get me to relax,' she snapped. 'Surprisingly.'

'Perhaps I'll remind you in a different way, then,'

Cristiano answered, and he turned her around to face him. Her eyes widened, lips parting instinctively as she gazed at him warily. Cristiano lowered his head, sensing every eye in the room upon them. Then he stroked that crimson mouth with one fingertip, felt Laurel's shuddering breath and smiled.

CHAPTER NINE

LAUREL FELT CRISTIANO's finger on her mouth and, despite her desperate determination not to react, to yield, fireworks started going off in her body. His other hand remained on her waist, fingers splayed over her hip, and she was more conscious of his hands touching her than she'd been of anything in her life.

She couldn't keep from responding, tilting her head back as he traced the outline of her lips, a move so seemingly innocent and yet so overwhelmingly sensual. Distantly she heard the ripple of murmurs around them, like waves breaking on a faraway shore.

Cristiano dropped his finger from her mouth, looking, of course, utterly unmoved besides a faint flush on his high, sharp cheekbones. 'Good girl,' he murmured and Laurel wanted to weep.

This felt so much worse than those awful moments with Bavasso, when she'd felt trapped and frozen by shock, caught in a drama in which she'd had no intention of acting. This felt as if her soul was being slowly and inexorably crushed. Every moment she stayed down here—draped on Cristiano's arm, 'mistress' practically branded on her forehead in scarlet letters—felt like a sacrifice, a slaying, of everything she was.

Because this wasn't who she was. Who she wanted to be. And the fact that she'd actually given herself to this man, and it had meant something to her, made her want to curl up in a ball and cry.

'Chin up,' Cristiano said, touching her chin with his finger. 'And smile.'

Laurel couldn't summon a smile. She turned away from him, conscious of the whispers, the murmurs, the looks. Was she imagining the derision? The contempt? A woman's lip curled and Laurel blinked back tears. She *hated* this.

'Drink,' Cristiano ordered, and handed her a flute of fizzing champagne. Laurel took a long swallow, needing the alcohol to dull her senses, which were heightened to a painful point.

'Easy,' he said, and her fingers tightened around the stem of the glass.

'Stop ordering me around,' she hissed. 'I'm an adult—not a puppet, not a doll, despite what you and everyone here believes.'

And, because she desperately needed some space, she stalked away from him, her dress swishing around her ankles, her head held high as she met no one's gaze.

She couldn't do this. She certainly couldn't do this for two whole weeks. Laurel took another sip of champagne and willed herself to get a grip. Two weeks and she could have her life, or at least most of her life, back...as long as she wasn't pregnant. And she couldn't be pregnant. She just couldn't be.

Out of the corner of her eye she saw a flash of red and her whole body stiffened. It was her mother, Elizabeth, standing alone in the corner of the casino.

Laurel walked towards her, a mix of despair and relief churning inside her.

'Elizabeth.' Her mother had never wanted her to call her Mom, or Mother, not even when Laurel had been small, although occasionally the endearment slipped out. It didn't now.

'Laurel.' Elizabeth's gaze was as conflicted as Laurel's, a mix of guilt and relief. 'I'm glad to see you safe.' Her mother's gaze raked her up and down. 'And it seems you landed on your feet.'

For a moment Laurel couldn't speak. Her chest burned with indignation and hurt and she simply stared, battling emotions too intense to verbalise. 'You call this *on my feet*?' she finally squeezed out. 'Did you…did you know Rico Bavasso was going to attack me?'

'Of course I didn't.' Guilt flashed across her mother's face again. 'Do you think I'd have let you upstairs if I'd known what he planned? I was expecting him to propose!'

For a second Laurel almost wanted to laugh. Her mother sounded outraged…on her own behalf.

'You must have suspected something,' she insisted in a low voice. 'The way he was acting on the casino floor…'

'What old man doesn't like to flirt with a beautiful young woman? Do you think I liked it? That I welcomed such an occurrence? He was mine.'

'He's not now?'

'I haven't seen him since. He wants nothing to do with me.' Elizabeth sounded more resigned than bitter. 'It was a bad idea, bringing you along. It just showed me up.'

'That's your takeaway from all of this?' Laurel let out a hollow laugh. Her mother had always been foremost concerned with herself. The only saving grace was that she was up front and unapologetic about it. *I spent the first twenty-four years of my life living for other people, wearing myself out. It's time I started thinking about myself.* And it seemed she'd never stopped.

Laurel shook her head, weary now. 'I never should have come here.'

'Who are you with now?' Elizabeth asked, ever pragmatic. 'Someone worth it, I hope?'

Laurel closed her eyes briefly. 'I'm with Cristiano.'

'Cristiano?' Elizabeth boggled at that bit of news. 'I thought he'd never have anything to do with either of us ever again.'

'And with good reason.'

'You know I never would have left Lorenzo.' Elizabeth's voice was tight. 'That money wasn't…'

'I know,' Laurel said tiredly, because she'd heard this all before. 'But it was still stealing.'

'We were married.' Elizabeth struggled to contain her bitterness, even after all these years. 'Can you blame me for wanting a nest egg?'

The trouble was, Laurel couldn't. Not exactly. But she couldn't justify it, either. So she said nothing, and Elizabeth's scarlet mouth twisted bitterly. 'Watch your back, that's all I have to say. Cristiano sold me down the river and he'll have no compunction doing the same to you.'

'Wait—what?' Laurel stared at her mother in surprised confusion. 'What do you mean, he sold you down the river?'

Elizabeth shrugged. 'He told Lorenzo about the bank account, fired him up and made it all seem far worse than it was.' She took a sip of her drink, a shadow of sorrow passing over her features. 'I did love him, you know—Lorenzo. No matter what his son or anyone else thought.'

'I know you did.' She'd doubted many things about her mother but not that. But Laurel hadn't realised it was Cristiano who had blown the whistle on her. Did it make a difference?

'Be careful,' Elizabeth said in a low voice. 'About Cristiano and about Rico. This isn't your world, Laurel. You're far too naïve for it. I shouldn't have dragged you into this, but I was desperate. I wanted to please Rico. I should have realised he'd prefer you.'

'I'm going to leave this world as soon as I can,' Laurel promised. 'All I want is to go home.'

'It won't be home for much longer, I'm afraid,' Elizabeth stated bluntly. 'I'll need my half.'

Cold crept into Laurel's bones, even though she'd been expecting this. Of course she had. 'But you said—'

'Laurel, I only agreed to give you my half of the house because I thought Rico was going to propose! I'm sorry, but I need the money.'

Laurel swallowed tightly. 'Please, Mom,' she whispered, using the endearment her mother never liked. Sometimes it slipped out, because she'd always wanted a mother. A proper mother, who cuddled, kissed and cared. 'Please. That house is the only thing...'

Elizabeth's expression turned sly. 'Maybe you can get something out of Cristiano. If you can, then we'll talk.'

Something out of Cristiano? He might have bought her these clothes but he wouldn't give her a penny. And she wouldn't ask for one. Laurel swallowed. 'You know that's impossible.'

'Then the house will have to be sold. Your grandfather left me half that house in his will. It's my inheritance as much as yours.'

'I know it is, but…'

A hand closed around Laurel's arm like a steel band, making her nearly drop her drink. 'As much as I hate to interrupt this little chat, we have places to be and people to see.' Cristiano inclined his head towards Elizabeth, his gaze glittering, before he steered Laurel away.

'You didn't have to—' she began, only to be cut off by his clipped voice.

'Bavasso is here.'

'Is he? Where?'

Cristiano nodded towards the baccarat table and Laurel's blood felt as if it had frozen in her veins as she caught sight of the man who had assaulted her last night: neatly dressed, the silver thatch of hair, the glinting eyes. A handsome older man, charming when he wanted to be, yet he made her skin crawl and her stomach heave.

The reaction was visceral, instinctive; she couldn't have controlled it if she'd tried. 'I think,' she whispered, 'I'm going to faint.'

Cristiano's arm came around her waist as Laurel sagged against him. 'Not yet, *bella*,' he murmured and then, as Bavasso turned to watch, he kissed her in front of everyone, his mouth moving over hers with possessive thoroughness, causing desire to flow through her, a molten river of want. Another moment and she'd be reduced to a puddle on the floor.

'Please,' Laurel whispered when he finally broke the kiss. 'I can't... I can't handle any more of this. Please get me out of here.'

Cristiano glanced at Bavasso and then, seemingly satisfied, he started walking towards the lifts. 'Very well. I think we've made our point.'

Laurel managed to keep herself upright as she walked past the staring crowds and saw Bavasso's tight expression, the bodyguards on either side of him. The lifts. All she needed to do was get through those gleaming black doors.

They opened and Laurel practically hurled herself inside. When they'd closed again she let out a sound that was halfway to a moan and crumpled against the wall, her knees buckling beneath her. It was the second time in the space of twenty-four hours that she'd fled to a lift. Her dress pooled around her as she slowly slid to a seated position, resting her head on her arms.

'Was it really so terrible?' Cristiano asked dryly. 'Being seen on my arm?'

'Everything about it was terrible.' Laurel drew a ragged breath, willing herself not to cry. She didn't think Cristiano would be impressed by her tears. 'I felt cheaper than I ever have in my life right then.'

'Cheaper than last night?' Cristiano demanded in disbelief, sounding annoyed. Laurel looked up, conscious of the tears pooling in her eyes and starting to streak down her cheeks. It seemed she was going to cry after all.

'Yes, Cristiano, cheaper. Because, although you'd never believe it, I wasn't trying to impress Bavasso.

He wasn't my *mark*.' Her voice hitched and she forced herself to continue. 'I was there to meet my mother's boyfriend, possibly fiancé, and when he started treating me… Well, you know how he treated me. I didn't know what to do. How to respond. And so I froze and I let it happen, and it made me feel awful, but *this*…' She swiped at her cheeks. 'I gave myself to you last night. I know it didn't mean anything to you, of course I do, but it meant something to me. Maybe it shouldn't have, but it did. And to be treated like your mistress, your possession, your *plaything*… I hated it. I hated every minute of it.'

She'd said way too much. Far more than she'd ever intended to reveal. Anything she said could and would be used against her, no doubt. She'd just given him ammunition, but she felt too weary and heartsick to care.

The doors opened and Laurel started to scramble to her feet, hampered by the long, narrow skirt of her gown. Cristiano reached a hand down to help her but Laurel jerked away.

'I don't need your help—'

'Don't be ridiculous,' he snapped, and helped her up. 'I don't think Bavasso will bother you, at any rate. If it's any consolation, I think he received the message we wanted him to.'

'It isn't,' Laurel tossed over her shoulder, and stalked into the penthouse.

Cristiano watched as Laurel kicked off her heels, her whole body trembling, and then started yanking the pins from her hair. It was what he'd wanted to do earlier, to dismantle the elaborate costume she was wearing, but now that she was the one doing it he felt annoyed somehow. There was no pleasing him when it came to this contrary woman, it seemed. And there was no pleasing her.

'I don't really understand what you're so upset about,' he said levelly as Laurel shook out her hair. She grabbed a tissue from the box and wiped at her lipstick, tears now drying on her face, leaving raccoon-like circles under her eyes.

'Of course you don't.'

'This is what we agreed on. The most expedient way to get you out of the mess you got yourself into. I'm *helping* you, Laurel.' And he wouldn't think about what she'd said about Bavasso flirting with her, how she'd frozen. It made sense, yet Cristiano resisted trusting Laurel, even that far. Trusting anyone.

'I know, I know.' She scrubbed at her lips until they were raw looking. 'You're a prince.'

He couldn't miss the sarcasm. As for the other things she'd said in the lift—about what they'd done last night meaning something to her—well, she'd been a virgin. Of course she was going to dress up what had been nothing more than a very pleasurable physical act. He'd been expecting it, but it didn't make it any easier to deal with.

Sighing, Cristiano reached for his phone. 'Why don't you change, since you apparently find that haute couture gown so abhorrent? And shower, if you like. I'll order us some food.'

She stared at him, a storm of emotion in her eyes, and then without a word she turned on her heel and stalked into the bedroom, slamming the door behind her.

Women. Muttering a curse, Cristiano dialled for room service.

Twenty minutes later the food had arrived and Laurel emerged from her bedroom dressed in a pair of loose linen pants and a silky T-shirt, her damp hair curling in ringlets about her face and shoulders. Cristiano liked her better this way, not that he would say it out loud. The last thing he wanted to do was give Laurel any hope for what could be between them.

Laurel's face was composed, nothing showing in her eyes. The emotional, distraught woman from before was replaced with someone who thankfully was calm and hopefully going to be sensible.

'What would you like to eat?'

'Anything is fine.' Laurel sank onto the sofa, curling her bare feet under her as she gazed out at the night sky. Her expression was pensive, and she didn't even look at Cristiano as he handed her a plate of food.

'Thank you,' she murmured.

'You're welcome.' Cristiano sat opposite her. 'What did your mother say to you down there, anyway?'

She turned to glance at him. Still nothing in her eyes, in her face. 'She wanted to know what had happened to me.'

'And what did you tell her?'

'Not much.' She leaned her head back against the sofa, looking so weary Cristiano had the impulse to comfort her. To reassure her—yet about what? 'Your kiss told her all she needed to know.' She spoke lifelessly, without any interest or spark.

'And last night with Bavasso?' He took a careful, even breath. 'Was it really...was it how you said?'

Laurel shrugged. 'Believe what you like.'

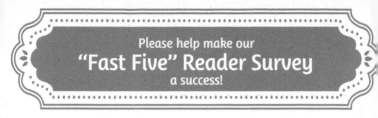

Dear Reader,

Since you are a lover of our books, your opinions are important to us... and so is your time.

That's why we made sure your **"FAST FIVE" READER SURVEY** can be completed in just a few minutes. Your answers to the five questions will help us remain at the forefront of women's fiction.

And, as a thank-you for participating, we'd like to send you **4 FREE THANK-YOU GIFTS!**

Enjoy your gifts with our appreciation,

Pam Powers

To get your
4 FREE THANK-YOU GIFTS:

✷ Quickly complete the "Fast Five" Reader Survey
and return the insert.

"FAST FIVE" READER SURVEY

1	Do you sometimes read a book a second or third time?	○ Yes ○ No
2	Do you often choose reading over other forms of entertainment such as television?	○ Yes ○ No
3	When you were a child, did someone regularly read aloud to you?	○ Yes ○ No
4	Do you sometimes take a book with you when you travel outside the home?	○ Yes ○ No
5	In addition to books, do you regularly read newspapers and magazines?	○ Yes ○ No

YES! I have completed the above Reader Survey. Please send me my 4 FREE GIFTS (gifts worth over $20 retail). I understand that I am under no obligation to buy anything, as explained on the back of this card.

❏ I prefer the regular-print edition
106/306 HDL GMVR

❏ I prefer the larger-print edition
176/376 HDL GMVR

FIRST NAME   LAST NAME

ADDRESS

APT.#   CITY

STATE/PROV.   ZIP/POSTAL CODE

READER SERVICE—Here's how it works:

'Last night you said it wasn't what it looked like. Is that why?' Her gaze slid away from his and Cristiano felt in his gut that there was more she wasn't saying. Laurel wasn't quite as innocent as she wanted him to think. 'Tell me the truth, Laurel.'

She sighed and picked at her food, her hair falling forward to hide her face. 'About a week ago my mother came to me and asked me for…for a favour, I suppose. We hadn't seen much of each other in recent years, or really at all. She'd been dating Rico Bavasso and she said he wanted to meet me.'

'What I saw last night was hardly your mother introducing you as her daughter to her boyfriend.' Cristiano couldn't keep the scepticism from his voice. He didn't even want to.

'I know. She said he was feeling his age and it would do him good to flirt with a younger woman. It sounded innocent, but maybe it was just me being naïve.' Laurel gulped. 'I can't believe my mother would…'

'Set you up?'

'She wanted him for herself.' Laurel shook her head. 'When I talked to her tonight, she was annoyed that Bavasso had been interested in me at all.'

'Charming.'

Laurel sighed. 'That's just how she is. I've accepted it.' She glanced up at him, something in her expression hardening. 'You don't know anything about my mother or me, for that matter. So please don't judge.'

'It's hard not to judge from what I saw and continue to see,' Cristiano returned coolly. 'What I don't understand is why you agreed to come at all, if there has been no love lost between the two of you.'

'Because I suppose I'm always hoping it will be better between us this time.' Laurel hesitated, and Cristiano waited for the other shoe to drop, because surely it would? 'And,' Laurel admitted quietly, 'Because she offered me something I wanted very much.'

There it was, just as Cristiano had known. His instincts hadn't been wrong. 'And what did you want so much?' he asked.

'A house. My house.' Cristiano stared at her, nonplussed, and Laurel continued, 'I spent a lot of my childhood at my grandfather's house in Canton Heights. It's a small farmhouse, nothing special, but I love it. It's the only place besides… Well, the only place I think of as home.'

'Besides?' Cristiano honed on that revealing word. 'Besides what?'

Laurel shrugged, her gaze sliding away. 'Besides the villa in Milan when we lived with your father. That felt like home, for a little while.'

Three years. He stared at her, trying to gauge what she was feeling. How much she was feeling. 'And so this house…' he said after a pause. 'Your mother agreed to…what? Give it to you?'

'Her half. My grandfather died three months ago and he left the house, the only thing he had, to both of us equally. I think he was hoping she'd come back, settle down.' She let out a humourless laugh. 'She'd never do that. My mother hates the place. But she agreed to sign over her half to me if I…met Bavasso and was nice to him. So I agreed, because the only thing I've ever wanted in life is my own house. My own home.' Her voice wobbled and she looked away.

'Why didn't you just offer to buy her out?'

Laurel let out a shaky huff of laughter. 'Because I don't have a hundred grand just sitting around,' she returned. 'Even farmhouses in rural Illinois cost money, you know. Money I don't have.'

Cristiano remained nonplussed. 'Still, you were agreeing to a rather large unknown just for a house.'

Laurel sucked in a breath, swinging around to stare at him, her face pale, her eyes narrowed. 'Says someone who has no idea what it's like not to have one.'

'What do you mean?'

'Oh, come on, Cristiano. You're rich. You've always been rich. You have absolutely no idea what it's like not to be. To be *poor*.'

He opened his mouth to make some suitably stinging reply and then closed it. She was right. He didn't know. He never had. 'That's true,' he said evenly. 'I don't.'

Laurel let out a tired laugh. 'But it doesn't excuse making reprehensible or at least stupid decisions. I know.'

'I didn't say that.'

'It was on your face. You might as well have shouted it.'

Could she read him so easily? Because, yes, he had been thinking something along those lines. He didn't particularly like Laurel knowing, though.

'If it makes any difference, it happened in increments,' Laurel said. 'I agreed to meet Bavasso as no more than my mother's boyfriend. And then we got to Rome and my mother was telling me to dress up for him. Okay, fine. And then it was "be nice to him", and I didn't even know what that meant. I think she felt trapped. She wanted him for himself, but she realised she'd lose him altogether if I wasn't…well.' She shook her head. 'She didn't mean for me to be hurt, that I do believe. Things got out of hand for both of us. But I'm not excusing any of it, trust me.'

'All right.' Cristiano absorbed all that for a moment before continuing, 'Tell me about your childhood.' Because he realised he wanted to know. 'Before your mother married my father. Where did you grow up?'

She looked surprised, then a little wary. 'Why do you want to know?'

'Perhaps it will help me to understand who you are and why you've made the choices you have. That can only be a good thing, surely, since we have to spend the next two weeks together?'

'By your decree.' Laurel sighed. 'Fine. Where should I begin?'

'Why not at the beginning?' Cristiano gave her a mirthless smile. 'It's the very best place to start.'

CHAPTER TEN

LAUREL SHIFTED ON the sofa, unsure how to deal with Cristiano's request. He wanted to know about her? Why? To use whatever she said against her? And yet she was so tired of staying suspicious. Being so careful all the time with him. And that tactic hadn't worked out all that well so far, so why not tell him everything? Who cared what he thought? He'd already shown her tonight what he thought of her—just another mistress. A prop.

Being seen on his arm—knowing what people were whispering about her, knowing what she and Cristiano had done together—it had been worse than anything she'd endured with Bavasso. More shameful. And she knew Cristiano would never understand that.

'My mother was born in rural Illinois,' she began. 'My grandfather was a poor farmer and they didn't have much money. She married a local boy and they had me.'

'Sounds like a fairly normal story so far.'

Oh, that even tone. The mildness. 'It was,' Laurel agreed, trying to match his tone. 'They struggled, but so did a lot of people. But then my father lost his job on the assembly line of a local factory. He started drinking too much. Things started to get ugly, or so my mother tells me. I was only four at the time, when he left.'

'Four? Do you remember your father?' He was looking at her closely, but she couldn't tell anything from his tone or his expression.

'Vaguely. The smell of chewing tobacco, the scratchiness of his shirt. Sitting next to him in his truck.' She shrugged, trying to ignore the tightness that had started in her throat and chest. 'It all feels like parts of an old dream. Foggy fragments, no more.'

'Yes.'

Something about the way he spoke, the contained feeling underneath the words, made her ask, 'What about your mother? Do you remember her?'

'Yes, of course. She died when I was nine.' Cristiano spoke dismissively, looking away, making Laurel wonder. 'So what happened after your father left?'

Laurel shrugged. 'My mother tried to get work but it was hard. Not much was going on in that part of Illinois, and of course she had me to take care of. My grandfather needed to work on the farm and my grandmother had died before I was born. We moved to Chicago and while she was waitressing she met someone.'

Her first 'daddy'. Laurel had always hated how Elizabeth made her call the men she'd entertained her father…except for the ones who weren't interested in kids. More than one boyfriend had never known about her at all. Laurel had been very good about staying quiet, hiding in cupboards, pretending she didn't exist.

'And that's how it began? Elizabeth funding her lifestyle through a series of men?'

'Yes, you could put it that way, I suppose.' Laurel sighed, disliking how scornful he sounded, although she couldn't really blame him. 'It was hard for her, you know. More than one of her boyfriends was bad news. Seriously bad news. Sometimes we had to run.'

And sometimes her mother would leave her with her grandfather in Canton Heights, which had been the sweetest relief, as well as a disappointment. No more dank hotel rooms or temporary apartments, no more late nights crouching in corners or under the covers. No more drama and endless uncertainty. And no more Mom.

But then her mother would always collect her again, and in her mother's sudden, desperate hug Laurel had believed Elizabeth did love her and want her with her. Why else would she come back for her? And there had been moments when Elizabeth had seemed, if not quite maternal, then at least a little caring. She'd given Laurel plenty of advice, a lot of it bitter, and when she'd landed Lorenzo she'd promised Laurel things would be better for her too. It wasn't much, but Laurel believed her mother loved her, in her own way. At least, she wanted to believe that.

'So you had ten years of this and then she hit the jackpot with my father.'

Laurel flinched a bit at his tone but then she lifted her chin and met his cool gaze head on. 'Yes, but you know she didn't even realise how rich he was when she met him.'

'She just got lucky, then.'

'Yes, I suppose she did. I know what it looks like—and, trust me, I know my mother is selfish and self-serving—but I do believe she and your father loved each other, Cristiano.' Her mouth twisted. 'Obviously that isn't something you can understand.'

He leaned forward, his eyes sparking gold fire. 'They loved each other? That's why she siphoned two million euros into her own private bank account?'

'She was trying to protect herself.' Laurel held up a hand. 'I *know* it was wrong. I'm not justifying it, just trying to make you understand. This is a woman who grew up dirt poor, who had men treat her badly time and time again. She was trying to give herself a little security—but, yes, I realise it was stealing.' Memory sharpened inside her. 'I didn't know you were the one who told your father, though.'

Something flickered in Cristiano's eyes. 'Why shouldn't I have?'

'I'm not saying you shouldn't have. Only...you could have asked her first. You could have tried to figure out what was going on.'

'It was fairly obvious, *bella*.'

'Don't call me *bella*!' Laurel snapped. 'Not now. Not ever.'

'I did what was right. Surely you can't deny that?'

'I just wished you'd talked to her first. I don't think she would have ever left him. She's lived her whole life on the edge. With Lorenzo we'd both finally found a haven. Your father was a kind man, Cristiano. If he'd been told another way, he might have understood.' Ten years later she still remembered her mother's resignation, felt her own numb shock at Lorenzo's cold treatment of them both. He'd taken her for rides in his sports car. He'd slipped her pocket money and tousled her hair. He'd bought her a dress for a school dance. He'd been more of a father to her than anyone, save her grandfather, and he'd cut her off without so much as a conversation. But that was a pain too deep and personal to share with Cristiano, especially when he was looking at her with such disdain.

'I cannot believe,' Cristiano said, ice in every word, 'That you are blaming me for what happened when your mother is so clearly a gold-digger and a thief.'

'I'm not blaming you. I just wished it could have been handled differently—'

'And,' he cut her off with even more arctic tones, 'I cannot believe you are defending the woman who as good as sold you to a man twice your age just twenty-four hours ago.'

Laurel looked away, blinking hard. She couldn't argue with what he said. Her mother had treated her badly, no matter what protestations she'd made earlier. Even if she believed what her mother had said… It was just that Laurel had always wanted to see the best in her mother. Wanted to believe her mother loved her, deep down. *Because if your own mother didn't love you…* 'I've already told you, I'm not defending her,' she said after a moment, her voice low. 'Just trying to explain things. Not that you'd accept any explanations.'

'Like I said, actions speak for themselves.'

'They do, don't they?' Laurel risked a look back at him, noting the flinty eyes, the granite jaw. He was completely unmoved. 'And yours do too. What made you so suspicious of people, Cristiano? Of women? Because you were suspicious of my mother from the moment you met her.'

'Of course I was. My father picked her up in a cheap casino in Palm Beach. They married in four days. Who wouldn't be suspicious?'

'A whirlwind romance.'

He let out a huff of humourless laughter. 'That's one way of putting it.'

'Still, it's more than that,' Laurel insisted. 'You're suspicious of everyone. Every woman, myself included. Why?'

He stared at her for a long moment. 'Life experience.'

'What life experience?'

She didn't think he'd answer but then he shifted restlessly on the sofa and bit out, 'After my mother died my father had several mistresses. They all took him for a ride. They were so patently false: the cloying way they spoke; pretending to be interested in me, a sulky ten-year-old.' He shook his head, the movement terse, angry. 'They were just out to get whatever they could—money, jewels, cars, clothes. They raked it in until my father realised they were using him and then he cut them off.'

'So we both endured a parade of other people in our lives,' Laurel said quietly. 'It's hard, but it doesn't need to make you cynical.'

'Cynical?' Cristiano challenged. 'Or smart? Before your mother my father married a woman. Jade. She was twenty-three, a bombshell. A *bomb*—and she detonated right in the middle of our lives. She took my father for nearly everything he had. He hadn't bothered with a pre-nuptial agreement, because he was so sure it was love.' Cristiano shook his head, his features twisting with the memory. 'Fortunately a lot of his money was tied up in property and unreachable to her. But she left him as destitute as she possibly could, and ran off with her boyfriend, who had been in on the whole thing.'

'I'm sorry,' Laurel said quietly. She heard the hurt in his voice but knew he wouldn't want her to try to comfort him. He'd hate the thought of her offering sympathy. Pity. Yet she understood him more than she ever had before. 'That's terrible,' she continued. 'But not everyone is like that.'

'None of this matters,' Cristiano dismissed. 'It has nothing to do with us.

'Us?' Laurel forced herself to ask, meeting his gaze directly, even though the look in his eyes felt as if it could freeze the blood in her veins. 'There is no "us".'

'There is if you're carrying my child.'

'Don't talk about that as if it is a probability.'

'It is a possibility.'

'Barely, and in any case you said we'd cross that unfortunate bridge if we came to it.'

'Very well,' Cristiano said evenly. 'Let's talk about the next two weeks.'

Laurel resisted the urge to shudder at the prospect of more evenings like the one she'd just endured. 'Are you going to drag me down to the casino again? Night after night?'

Cristiano's mouth twisted. 'You make it sound like a fate worse than death.'

'No, but it's not something I'm looking forward to in the slightest.'

Cristiano sat back, his gaze turning worryingly speculative. 'No, I don't think we'll go down there again,' he said slowly. 'I don't think Bavasso is a threat any more. He knows you're mine.'

Laurel eyed him warily, hating how arrogant he sounded. How possessive. She really was just a thing to him. An object to be used. 'What, then?' she asked.

'We'll go to France.'

'France?' Laurel's eyes widened almost comically. Cristiano sat back and smiled, glad to have surprised her. Because she'd surprised him too much already, with her anger and her hurt, and then her revelations about her childhood. Cristiano had told himself not to feel sorry for her, not to be moved by what was really a common-or-garden sob story, but he did. He pictured a very young Laurel hiding from one of her mother's abusive boyfriends and felt a boiling anger surge through his veins. And that was a very inconvenient thing to feel.

'Why would we go to France?'

'Because I have a new manager at my hotel in Paris and I want to check up on her. Also, there is a charity gala I am meant to attend. You can come as my date.'

'Your date?' Laurel was still goggling at him. 'But why? Bavasso won't be there.'

'I don't care about Bavasso any longer, and you shouldn't either. I need a date, and you're here. It's convenient.'

'So glad to be of service.' Laurel sat back, looking nonplussed by the change of plans. Cristiano understood her surprise. He'd only just decided to take her to Paris tonight. To escape the oppressive feeling here, with Bavasso below, her mother in attendance, all the bad memories swirling around them.

They'd go somewhere new, somewhere different, where the past didn't dog them. Where they could simply be and enjoy each other. Because all evening a realisation had been coalescing inside him—he wasn't done with Laurel Forrester. Their affair *would* be real, and therefore all the more convincing. But first he needed to explain the parameters.

He gazed at her now—the long, golden-brown curls, the shadowed eyes, the way she nibbled her lip. She was nervous, uncertain, maybe even afraid. He needed to reassure her. He also needed to convince her.

'Laurel.' She jerked her startled gaze towards him, eyes wide with wary apprehension. Cristiano leaned forward, his attention fully focused on the woman before him. 'What you said in the lift—about sex meaning something to you.'

Colour flared in her cheeks. 'Don't use that against me now,' she said. 'I didn't mean it like that.'

'Like what?'

She lifted her chin, a brave attempt at haughtiness. 'You don't need to worry that I'm going to fall in love with you, Cristiano. Trust me on that.'

This was unexpected, and for some reason her lofty assurance rubbed him the wrong way. 'What a relief.'

'I'm sure it is, since you seem to have an allergic reaction to love or commitment.'

'An allergy suggests something that isn't a choice,' Cristiano returned lightly. 'And trust me, Laurel, it is very much a choice.'

'Is it? Or is it just a reaction to your childhood, all those women of your father's?'

Cristiano sat back against the sofa and folded his arms. 'My, what a stunning little piece of psycho-analysis.'

'Actually, it seems fairly obvious to me. We're all products of our childhood, aren't we?' Laurel shrugged. 'I know I am.'

And now, even though he knew he shouldn't be, he was curious. He needed to know more. 'What do you mean by that?'

'People leave,' Laurel stated starkly. 'Don't they? Some by choice, some not. It's one of the reasons why I won't fall in love with you, Cristiano. I don't want to fall in love with anyone.'

'One of the reasons?'

A faint, sardonic smile curved her lush mouth. 'It's not exactly as if you've been Prince Charming, is it?'

'I… I…' He was actually stuttering in his shock. Suddenly she looked so smugly confident, sitting curled up on his sofa, acting as if the prospect of her falling for him was the remotest of possibilities. And yes, that was fine, that was what he wanted; of course it was. Yet he still found it seriously annoyed him.

'Thank you for putting me so much at my ease,' he said dryly when he'd thankfully recovered his composure. 'What, then, did you mean in the lift?'

She didn't pretend to misunderstand. 'Sex is important. You're giving yourself to someone, making yourself vulnerable. I mean, just being naked is being vulnerable, isn't it?' Cristiano shrugged a non-answer. He was, he realised with a pang of unease, out of his depth. He didn't talk about this kind of stuff. He didn't even think about it.

'And then the things you do together…' Her cheeks were going from pink to fiery red and Cristiano knew she was recalling all they'd done together. All he intended they do again. And again. 'Well, it means something. Not love, necessarily, but there's a bond of sorts. A shared memory. I know men seem able to dismiss it as just some kind of physical workout, but it didn't feel that way to me.'

'So,' Cristiano asked after a moment, the restless ache of desire surging through him as her words sparked memories of deep kisses and golden skin, 'what did it feel like to you?'

'Like I said, there's a bond.' Laurel's face was still red as she looked away. 'No matter what—even if I never see you again after these two weeks, which is the most likely scenario—there will be a bond. You… you were my first.'

The simply spoken words pierced him with guilt. Her first, and so far her only lover. It was a responsibility he hadn't wanted but, now he had it, and he wasn't going simply to throw it away.

'Then there's no reason not to make the most of these two weeks,' he said, and Laurel jerked around to face him, her mouth dropping open in shock.

'What…?'

'We gave each other a great deal of pleasure, Laurel. Surely you won't try to deny that?'

She gulped. Audibly. 'No, I can hardly deny that part of it.'

'And you have so kindly assured me that there is no risk of an emotional attachment. The bond we have is physical, and it's one we should both enjoy for as long as we can. Don't you think?'

'I…' She licked her lips and Cristiano could not keep from groaning at the sight.

'It seems you are doing your best to convince *me*,' he said, and her gaze widened, pupils flaring.

'I'm not trying to…'

'You don't need to try, *bella*.' He slipped off the

sofa and came to kneel before her. 'It just is.' He slid his hands along her legs, over her knees and across her thighs. Laurel shuddered in response. 'This thing between us—it just is. Why should either of us fight it?'

She stared at him, her pupils dilated, her breathing ragged. 'So two weeks of…of being together? That's what you want?' She breathed.

'It's very simple, isn't it? We enjoy each other and we both walk away satisfied.' He stroked her inner thighs lightly. 'Very satisfied.'

She stared at him, transfixed, a rosy flush sweeping over her whole body. Cristiano slid his hands higher, splaying his palms across the tops of her thighs, keeping her in place. Laurel let out a breathy little sigh, the sound of acceptance. Of victory.

Cristiano leaned in. 'We both want this, Laurel.'

Her eyes fluttered closed, her body trembling under his light touch. 'I… I know.'

'There's nothing to fear or regret here,' he added, compelled to reassure her even now. 'Nothing but pleasure for both of us.'

She nodded, the movement jerky, and Cristiano closed the space between their mouths. The kiss was deep and endless, branding them both. His hands tightened on her thighs, and hers gripped his shoulders, both of them steadying and anchoring each other.

Eventually, breathless and wanting, Cristiano broke the kiss. 'Yes?' he demanded, his voice raw with need.

Laurel opened her eyes and gazed at him, her expression both dazed and resolute. 'Yes,' she whispered.

CHAPTER ELEVEN

LAUREL WOKE UP to dazzling sunlight and an empty bed. She stretched, muscles aching that had never ached before. Hours later and she still felt sated and boneless. One thing was inarguable—Cristiano was an attentive, thorough and excellent lover.

Not, of course, that she had any way to measure his performance besides her own breathless satisfaction. She rolled onto her side, tucking her knees up to her chest and fought the expected rush of guilt and doubt. She'd made a decision last night, a foolhardy and potentially dangerous decision. Cristiano Ferrero was way, way out of her league. She didn't have any experience with dating, with men, with relationships.

But this wasn't a relationship.

A timely reminder, and one she would have to give herself constantly over the forthcoming days. No matter what she'd assured Cristiano last night, it would be all too easy to fall in love with him, or at least believe that she had. Because she might have told Cristiano she didn't want to fall in love with anyone, but that wasn't strictly true. It was simply that she hadn't yet found anyone to fall in love with. Anyone to take that almighty risk for—the risk of offering herself wholly with the possibility of being pushed away. People left. It was the one truth she'd learned over and over, yet she still kept hoping there was someone out there who wouldn't. Someone who would think she was worth staying for. She believed it because she wanted to believe she was lovable.

But she knew Cristiano wasn't the man who would convince her of that. So she'd take these two weeks and get out of them what she could. Because fighting Cristiano was a lost cause, especially when she was fighting herself as well, her own impossible desires and dreams. Far easier, and far, far more enjoyable, to give in.

And what a sweet surrender it had been.

Sighing, she stretched and then sat up in bed. She didn't know what the day held, or what Cristiano would act like now she truly was his lover. His mistress.

The door to the bedroom opened and Laurel stilled, before drawing the sheet up to cover herself. Cristiano stood in the doorway freshly showered and dressed with two cups of coffee.

'Good morning.'

'Good morning.' Laurel took the cup of coffee he handed her, cradling the warm mug between her palms.

'We leave for Paris in a couple of hours.'

'So soon?'

'I need to meet with my manager before the gala tonight.'

Laurel nodded slowly and took a sip of coffee. 'All

right.' She was excited to go to France, to escape the confines of Rome and its recently made memories. She wanted to be somewhere new with Cristiano.

He turned away, his eyes narrowed as he gazed out at the bright sunshine of a summer's morning, at the light glinting off the windows and roofs of Rome; he looked so impossibly beautiful, the stark lines of his body and face gilded in sunlight.

'Cristiano.' Laurel's voice wavered and he turned, dark eyebrows raised in query. 'Thank you.'

A tiny smile quirked his mouth. 'Now, that was unexpected.'

'I know I haven't been particularly grateful for your intervention,' Laurel allowed with a small, answering smile. 'But I am. I don't know what I would have done if you hadn't stepped in.'

Something flashed across Cristiano's face, an emotion Laurel couldn't gauge, and then he gave a little nod. 'You should get dressed,' he said, and walked from the room.

An hour later Laurel stepped into the lift that would bring them to the lobby and the waiting limo to take them to the airport. She wore a shift dress in aquamarine linen and a pair of taupe open-heeled sandals, her hair caught back with a sapphire clip—and Laurel suspected the sapphires were real. It had come with a drawerful of jewellery that she was afraid to touch. Was this how Cristiano treated all his mistresses—with jewels, clothes and careless expense? She'd been telling herself all morning just to go with it, enjoy the over-the-top craziness, but she still found it hard.

She'd paid her own way since she was eighteen years old, working her way through her nursing degree with part-time jobs, insisting on paying rent—admittedly, a minimal one—to her grandfather. She didn't like feeling bought.

And yet she couldn't keep a warm glow from spreading through her when Cristiano saw her, a slow smile stealing over his features as his gaze swept over her. 'You look lovely.'

'Thank you,' Laurel murmured.

They now had a relationship of sorts and, while it felt far better than the constant battling, it was still... odd. Considering she'd never even had a boyfriend, Laurel was not at all sure how to navigate a love affair, and a temporary one at that.

Cristiano helped her into the limo and Laurel slid into the sumptuous leather luxury, amazed all over again at the turn her life had taken. In Illinois she drove an old pick-up truck.

'You look so surprised,' Cristiano remarked as he sat next to her, sliding out his phone and thumbing a few buttons.

'It's been a long time since I've been in a limo.'

He looked up, arching an eyebrow. 'How long?'

'Since our parents were married,' Laurel admitted. 'Those three years were like a dream to both of us. I think we knew it couldn't last.'

'Because your mother got greedy.'

'Let's not rehash this, Cristiano,' Laurel said on a sigh. 'I know what she did was wrong, okay?'

She couldn't help but wonder about the *what ifs*, though—what if he hadn't said anything about that bank account; what if Lorenzo and Elizabeth had stayed married… It beggared belief how different her life might have been now.

Except here she was in Italy, in a limo, living a life of luxury, if only for a short time,. So it seemed she had that life, albeit temporarily, after all.

'So what exactly are we doing in Paris?' she asked once they were settled in the first-class section on the plane, their seats forming a private nook.

'As I told you, I have a business meeting this afternoon, and then the charity gala tonight. After that…' His slow smile was like a burn, the wicked glint in his eyes a hiss. 'After that we can do what we like,' he murmured, his gaze lowering to sweep meaningfully over her.

And even though part of her felt she should resist the innuendo, the expectation, Laurel couldn't keep from reacting. Heat flared, need tightening inside her into sharp, aching points.

She smiled and looked away, trying to regain her composure. A flight attendant brought them both glasses of fizzing champagne, and Laurel took a much-needed sip. She wasn't much of a one for alcohol, but right now she needed the distraction.

'Relax,' Cristiano murmured as he lounged back in his seat and sipped his drink. 'Bavasso has been dealt with.'

But it wasn't Bavasso making her feel as if everything inside her was on edge. It was this man right here, his silvery gaze slipping inside her, stirring things up, making her restless, wanting and afraid.

After years of living a small, calm life, it felt like too much. Maybe, Laurel reflected wistfully, she just wasn't mistress material.

Cristiano watched Laurel fidget out of the corner of his eye and wondered why she was so nervous. It couldn't be Bavasso, so it had to be him and the new status of their relationship—although he used that word with caution.

Still, the last twelve hours had been some of the most enjoyable of his life. Not just the sex, which had been as incredible as before, but—dared he even think of it?—the company. He was starting to *like* Laurel— her feistiness, her sense of humour, her easy-to-read emotions and limitless compassion—something he'd never felt for any of his other mistresses, whose personalities had been of zero interest to him.

'What is the gala tonight in aid of?' Laurel asked. 'Which charity?'

'A children's hospice, I believe.'

'Really?' Interest sparked in her eyes. 'I'm a hospice nurse. Palliative care.' Which meant she helped people in the last days and weeks, even hours, of their lives.

'That must be difficult sometimes,' he said quietly.

'Yes, it can be. Sad, of course.' She gave a sorrowful smile. 'But it's often an overlooked part of the medical profession. People are so focused on getting better, they don't want to think about what happens when you can't.'

'Of course,' Cristiano murmured. He was disconcertingly moved by the thought of her helping people at such a hard time in their lives. The selflessness of it, when there was so little reward. The patients she dealt with were never going to get better. 'So how did you choose that particular field of nursing?' he asked, even though his gut was telling him to stop asking questions. *Stop being interested; stop caring, for heaven's sake.*

'My grandfather.' Laurel was quiet for a moment, her expression pensive and a little shadowed. 'He was diagnosed with dementia while I was doing my degree. I was living with him, working during the day and taking classes at night. My grandad really wanted to be able to stay at home as long as he could, and so I went even more part-time to make that happen. After all he'd done for me over the years...' She pressed her lips together, her gaze distant. 'It was the very least I could do.'

The very least, and yet so much. And, Cristiano reflected, the opposite of what he'd assumed. When she'd walked into the casino he'd decided right then that she was a shallow, mercenary, experienced gold-digger like her mother. Instead he was discovering how innocent she was, how *pure*. A woman who'd been willing to put her own ambitions aside to care for an elderly man; to dedicate her life to easing the burdens and sorrows for others.

It was an uncomfortable realisation.

'And you said your grandfather died three months ago?' he asked after a moment.

Laurel nodded. 'Yes, in the hospice where I work, so I could see him every day. That was a great blessing.' She let out a soft, sad sigh. 'And it was a great loss. The last year of his illness, he was very confused.

And the last few months, he didn't even know who I was.' Grief flashed across her face and then was gone.

Cristiano felt a tightening in his chest, an overflow of emotion. He was discovering depths to Laurel that amazed and humbled him. And, damn it, he still wanted her to be shallow. He needed her to be, because that was so much simpler. So much easier.

'I'm sorry,' he said again, the words heartfelt, but feeling useless.

'Thank you. I still miss him. I suppose I always will.' She turned to him with a small smile. 'Enough of my sob story,' Laurel said, injecting a note of brightness into her voice. 'What about you?'

What about him? What could he say? He was a sinner to her saint. At that moment, he felt he'd done nothing of note in his life whatsoever. Cristiano shifted in his seat and took a sip of champagne. 'What do you want to know?'

'How did you get started in the hotel business? Your father is in finance, isn't he?'

'Yes, he was. He's retired now.'

'So why hotels instead of the family business?'

'Because I wanted to be my own man, on my own terms, not just follow in my father's footsteps.' He hadn't wanted to follow in his father's footsteps in any way—not the business, not the three marriages, not the endless loop of love and heartbreak that had left his father alone and wistful in his villa in Capri, still hoping for some kind of silver years romance.

'Fair enough,' Laurel answered. 'So why hotels?'

Cristiano shrugged. 'I got my start by buying up a run-down *pensione* and turning it into an exclusive boutique hotel.' He shrugged. 'A combination of luck, risk and a small amount of skill.'

'I'm sure it was more than a small amount,' Laurel said, smiling, and Cristiano looked away.

'Maybe.' The truth was he'd been in the right place at the right time, and had been willing to take a risk on a big vision no one else had shared. It didn't feel like that much, all of a sudden.

'And from that one little *pensione* you now have how many hotels?' Laurel asked, and Cristiano turned back to her.

'An even dozen. Most are in Europe, but I'm expanding into North American and Asia.'

'With one in New York and one in Hong Kong.'

Cristiano arched an eyebrow. 'You're well informed.'

Laurel blushed and ducked her head. 'I read about it in the papers.'

'Did you?' That was interesting. Had she been keeping tabs on him? That schoolgirl crush from ten years ago had perhaps lain dormant. Once that information might have alarmed him, but now he felt strangely pleased by the thought.

'You are in the tabloids a lot, you know,' Laurel said, clearly trying to recover. 'With whatever supermodel or actress you're with at that nanosecond.'

'Nanosecond?' Cristiano leaned forward. 'That's insulting to my sexual prowess.'

Laurel's blush, which had faded to a lovely, dusky pink, now returned to red. 'I didn't mean it like that.'

'I know you didn't. You couldn't possibly have.' He leaned a little closer, so his leg nudged hers and his breath fanned her ear. 'But perhaps I need to remind you of it anyway.'

Laurel's lips parted soundlessly and her gaze darted around the first-class area. Their seats formed a private alcove, but it wasn't *that* private. Not private enough to do what Cristiano was now aching to do.

And yet... He trailed one hand up Laurel's bare leg, skimming the sensitive skin under her knee before sliding his fingers under the hem of her dress.

'Cristiano.' Laurel looked scandalised but also excited. He saw it in the flared pupils, the parted lips, heard it in her uneven breathing. And felt it in himself. He was barely touching her, yet it felt like the most wildly exciting thing he'd ever done.

He stroked the silky-smooth skin of her inner thigh, listening to her breathing hitch and feeling his own painfully intense reaction as lust arrowed through him.

'Someone will see,' Laurel whispered, her breath hitching, but she didn't move.

'See what?' Cristiano stroked her thigh again, letting his fingers slide just that little bit higher. Her skin felt like cool silk. 'We're just sitting here, chatting.' And, from the outside, that indeed looked like all they were doing. Their bodies blocked the view of Cristiano's hand where it was inching inexorably higher.

'Maybe, but...' Laurel shifted, giving him greater access—intentionally or not? Cristiano didn't know and he wondered if Laurel even knew. This was new territory for her and, he was realising more and more, new territory for him. Which made him all the more determined to put their relationship back onto familiar footing. Incredible sex and nothing more.

'But what?' Cristiano prompted softly. His fingers climbed higher, to the warm apex of her thighs, and Laurel let out a shuddering gasp as he stroked her knowingly.

'But…' Her voice trailed away as her eyes fluttered closed and she slouched in her seat, helpless to do anything but respond to his touch. Desire and triumph roared through him in a primal, possessive wave.

'But nothing,' Cristiano murmured as he continued to stroke. 'Nothing but this.'

'May I refresh your champagne?'

The bright, chirpy voice of the flight attendant had Laurel freezing, her eyes snapping open as she stared at the woman in shock, sprawled in her seat, her legs parted.

Cristiano withdrew his hand and straightened, giving the woman a smile as he reached for his glass. 'Why not?' he said. They could finish what they'd started when they reached Paris. Although his body ached with the need to slake himself with Laurel, he knew the few hours of delaying satisfaction would be a delicious torment for them both.

Laurel straightened, pulling her dress down, then taking a sip of her champagne, clearly trying to restore her composure. 'Do you do that kind of thing very often?' she asked unsteadily, and Cristiano hesitated.

Was she going to be jealous about the other women he'd had, insecure because of his experience and the lack of her own? But if he admitted that he hadn't done this before—that he never did anything that threatened his control of a situation, that she was the only one who made him act in a way he never would have expected—would she then assume that she was different from all the rest? That he would be different with her?

'Not very often,' he answered with a wicked smile and took a sip of champagne. Laurel nodded and sipped her own champagne, and Cristiano could tell his answer disappointed her, if just a little.

But it was important to remind her that this was an affair, two weeks of fantastic sex and absolutely no strings. Hell, Cristiano acknowledged moodily as he drained his glass, it seemed he needed the reminder as well.

CHAPTER TWELVE

LAUREL GAZED OUT of the window of her bedroom in the hotel suite of La Sirena, Paris as twilight settled softly over the City of Lights. They'd arrived several hours ago, and from the moment she'd stepped off the plane to now she'd been pampered, indulged and, yes, made love to.

They'd taken a limo from the airport to the hotel, and then the concierge had personally escorted them to the luxurious suite that Cristiano reserved for his personal use. As soon as the door had closed behind him, Cristiano had reached for her, kissing her hungrily as if it had been months rather than mere hours since they'd last been together.

And yet Laurel was hungry for him, ravenous, especially after the appetiser he'd teased her with on the plane. Just the memory of his knowing fingers climbing higher while people near them read newspapers or sipped champagne made Laurel blush and fidget. It had been utterly thrilling.

In the hotel suite he'd backed her towards the bedroom, tugging down the zip of her dress in one fluid movement and then helping her step out of it without missing a single stride. Laurel had walked backwards slowly, wearing only her bra and pants, her eyes glued to Cristiano as he unbuttoned his shirt and shrugged out of it.

She didn't think she'd ever tire of looking at him: the ridged muscles of his abdomen; the bronzed, burnished skin; the flare of heat in those silvery eyes. She could hardly believe that a man like this, a man who radiated such a powerful sexual charisma, wanted *her*.

Yet as he'd stalked her towards the bedroom, a predator intent on his more than willing prey, she knew he did.

He'd caught her up as she crossed the threshold, her breath coming out in a whoosh as their bodies made exquisite contact, hard against soft. Cristiano had made short work of her bra and pants, and then neatly hooked his leg behind her knees, so she'd had no choice but to fall onto the bed with a tremulous laugh.

He'd fallen with her, his body covering hers, so hot and hard and muscular. Legs, lips, hands, hips—all tangling, pressing, invading, *consuming*.

Just the memory of it all made Laurel's whole body tingle. If she'd known how fantastic sex could be, she'd have had it a whole lot sooner. Except, of course, she'd never met anyone she'd been remotely interested in taking that step with. She'd never met anyone like Cristiano.

A light knock sounded on the door. 'Ready, *bella*?' Cristiano called and Laurel turned to inspect her reflection in the mirror one last time.

She wore a royal-blue evening gown with off-the-shoulder straps and a diamanté belt encircling her waist, the gauzy material falling in a perfect column before pooling about her feet. A stylist had done her

hair in an artful up-do, with a few curls resting provocatively on her shoulders, and another assistant had
done her make-up, making her eyes look smoky, her
lashes endless. She looked elegant but also sexy, and
not, she hoped, like nothing more than Cristiano's latest. Tonight she did not want to be dismissed as the
eye candy on Cristiano's arm. And she didn't want
him to treat her that way, either.

Yet…she couldn't quite banish the memory of the
rest of the afternoon—the way Cristiano had quickly
rolled off the bed, pulling on his trousers and shirt
while Laurel had lain there, dazed and naked, the last
of her climax still thrumming through her.

'Where are you going?' she'd asked sleepily.

'I told you, I have a meeting.' Cristiano had reached
for his neck tie without looking at her. 'You can relax
here. Feel free to order anything you want from room
service.' He'd shot her a glinting smile. 'Too bad I'm
not on the menu.'

And then he'd gone, the door clicking shut behind
him, leaving Laurel alone for the rest of the afternoon.
There was no reason to feel lonely, she'd told herself
as she'd strolled through the sumptuous suite and then
indulged in a long, lovely bubble bath. No reason to
feel as if Cristiano was fobbing her off, putting her
in her place. This was what she'd signed up for, what
she'd agreed to. She was his mistress. This was what
mistresses did.

But for a little while, sitting in the suite alone, pick-
ing at the sandwich she'd ordered from room service,
she'd longed to go back to Illinois—to her grandfather's
house, to her job, to a life that made sense and made
her feel useful and important—admittedly, in a small

way, instead of lounging about like some useless ornament, waiting on Cristiano's pleasure.

'*Bella.*' Cristiano's voice was lazy with a hint of laughter as he rapped on the door again, startling Laurel out of her reflections. 'At this rate we're going to miss dinner.'

Laurel took a deep breath and banished those memories. Two weeks. Two weeks and then she would go back to that life, small and important as it was. She just needed to enjoy what she had and not ask for more. Not expect it to be different. 'I'm coming.'

Laurel opened the door, a purely feminine pride stealing through her at the look of blatant heat in Cristiano's eyes. It still amazed her that she affected him this way, just as he affected her. As always, he looked devastating in a tuxedo, the perfect foil to his ink-black hair and olive complexion.

'You look wonderful,' he said, the thrum of sincerity audible in his voice, then he took her hand and led her to the lifts.

The charity gala was being held in the hotel's opulent ballroom, a room with frescoed walls and giant crystal chandeliers, now filled with a crowd of the most elegant people Laurel had ever seen. For a second she hung back, overawed by it all, but Cristiano tugged on her fingers and brought her into the room.

'Remember,' he murmured. 'You're with me.'

He joined a group of business associates, wealthy men and women and their partners, everyone speaking in flawless French that Laurel couldn't follow. She spoke a smattering of Italian, thanks to her three years living in Milan, and a bit of schoolgirl French, but that was it. Everyone here seemed as if they spoke several languages with ease.

A middle-aged man turned to her with a friendly smile. 'Are you English?' he asked in accented English and Laurel smiled, grateful for someone making a friendly overture.

'American, actually. And I'm sorry, but I don't speak much French.'

'I speak English,' the man replied with a very Gallic shrug. 'So it is okay. You are with Monsieur Ferrero?' His inquisitive gaze flicked to Cristiano, who was engaged in a discussion with another businessman, but Laurel had the sense that he was listening intently to their conversation, even though he didn't so much as look at them.

'Yes. But I'm interested in hospice care,' she said, determined to be there on her own terms as much as she could. 'Back in the US, I work as a nurse in palliative care.'

'Do you?' The man's eyes sparked with interest. 'I would love to hear your thoughts about rehabilitative palliative care. Do you practise that where you work?'

'We are beginning to,' Laurel said with real enthusiasm. It was invigorating to talk to someone about issues that mattered, to feel useful again, with more to contribute than simply being an accessory or a clothes horse. 'It's difficult, because of course you have to reach patients earlier, before they're referred to hospice care.'

'Exactly. We are pioneering a new method, of consultants giving us referrals of anyone with a non-curative diagnosis.'

'But most people don't want to hear they have a

non-curative diagnosis,' Laurel said quietly. 'They want to believe they can get better.'

'Yes.' The man nodded and then extended his hand. 'Michel Durand, consultant at the Institut Curie.'

'Laurel Forrester. A nurse at Canton Heights General Hospital.' She gave a self-conscious smile as she shook his hand.

They chatted for a few more minutes, with Laurel becoming increasingly animated as Michel asked her opinion on various new initiatives in palliative care happening in America. Then he glanced at Cristiano, eyebrows raised.

'Do you mind if I steal your lovely companion away for a few minutes? There are a few people here I'd like her to meet.'

Cristiano's expression was suspiciously bland as he smiled and nodded. 'Of course.'

With one quick, questioning look which Cristiano returned just as blandly, Laurel went.

Cristiano tracked Laurel's progress across the crowded ballroom as he half-listened to one of his associates drone on about an investment opportunity in Bucharest.

'It's ripe for tourist venues, and there's a lovely nineteenth-century building perfect for renovation, right in the heart of the Old Town…'

'La Sirena Bucharest?' Cristiano dragged his gaze away from Laurel to give the man a small smile. 'I'll think about it.'

Then he turned back with narrowed eyes to watch Laurel laugh and chat with several men who, improbably, were not staring at her cleavage but actually listening to what she was saying.

And she must have been saying something important, because she looked so passionate—eyes sparkling, mouth curving, her hands moving in graceful arcs as she described something. Cristiano had no idea what, but he couldn't look away from her. And neither could any of her listeners.

What was the emotion churning like acid in his gut? Was it a simple matter of jealousy? His mistresses were *his*. They devoted their time and attention to him. It was so obvious that he'd never needed to articulate it in one of his arrangements. But his arrangement with Laurel was like no other.

'Who is she?'

Cristiano turned to see the man who had suggested the Bucharest hotel—Niko Savakis—nodding towards Laurel. 'Your latest *amour*,' he clarified, making Cristiano inexplicably want to punch him. 'Who is she?'

'Her name is Laurel Forrester.'

'She's different from your usual blonde bombshells,' Savakis remarked.

'Oh?' Cristiano's voice was dangerously quiet. 'How is that?' He did not like Savakis looking at Laurel as if she was something one purchased in a shop. He didn't, he realised, like Savakis thinking of Laurel as simply his mistress, here today, most likely gone tomorrow.

None of this made any sense.

'She's intelligent and articulate, for one,' Savakis replied mildly. 'She's beautiful, but not in a showy, obvious, clearly fake way.' He gave Cristiano an amused glance. 'Not to disparage your previous mistresses, of course. But Miss Forrester certainly seems like a cut above. Perhaps you'll hold onto her for a while.'

'Perhaps I will.'

Savakis registered Cristiano's even tone with a little amused smile. 'And if you don't... I'm sure there are plenty of men who would happily take your place.' His considering gaze flicked back to Laurel; she was laughing, looking incandescent and so very happy. 'Myself included.'

'Don't even think about it,' Cristiano warned him in a low growl. His fists bunched at his sides. Savakis looked surprised, and then he smiled.

'So she is different,' he murmured, and moved away.

Cristiano forced himself to relax. *What was going on here?* This was not how he conducted relationships. Affairs. *Arrangements.* He didn't care about the women he was with. He barely thought about them beyond what they could provide in bed.

Laurel was different. And, even more alarmingly, he was different with Laurel.

Since she'd stumbled into his penthouse just three days ago she'd shaken him up. Reached him in a way no one else had, and certainly not a woman he'd slept with. He didn't understand it. Didn't understand himself. And he hated not feeling as if he was in control—of the situation and of himself.

But one thing he knew more than any other was that he was not happy with her across the room, chatting and laughing, looking as if she was having the time of her life. Without him.

With each step cementing his purpose, Cristiano strode across the room to join Laurel.

'Ah, Ferrero.' Michel Durand, the doctor who had spirited Laurel away, gave Cristiano what seemed a too-knowing smile. 'Where did you find such a charming and intelligent woman? She is far from your usual date.'

Did everyone have to keep mentioning the attributes, or lack thereof, of his usual paramours? Cristiano smiled tightly. 'She found me, as it happens.'

Laurel blushed and Durand glanced between them both, intrigued. 'Is that so? It sounds as if there's a story there.'

'There is,' Cristiano agreed smoothly, inserting himself into the little circle and sliding his arm around Laurel's waist. 'But it is not one I am going to tell you.'

'Ah.' Durand looked again between them, his gaze sliding speculatively from Laurel to Cristiano and then back again. 'Very intriguing. We have been having a most illuminating conversation about rehabilitative care.'

'A very important topic, I am sure.' And one he knew nothing about. After a tiny pause the conversation started up again, swirling around him. He could hardly contribute, save for the generous cheque he would write for the hospice—that was something he was good for, at any rate.

But after a few moments of battling his own petty irritation Cristiano started to listen. He listened to Laurel's impassioned plea for dignity in end-of-life care, and was amazed—although he acknowledged there was no real reason to be so surprised—at how articulate she was. How determined and passionate. And he felt something stir inside him, something that had been long and purposefully dormant.

It was strange and unsettling, this awakening inside him, parts of his soul stirring to life, his atrophied heart stretching and seeking. It was strange and deeply alarming, because he didn't want to start caring about Laurel. Yet since she'd catapulted back into his life he'd been battling against just that.

If he was smart, he would let her go. Tell her to have a nice life and send her back to Illinois. But Cristiano knew he couldn't do that. First, because she might be pregnant, and second, because he didn't want to.

The second reason trumped the first by a long shot.

During a lull in the conversation, Laurel caught him looking at her and she smiled uncertainly. 'Why are you scowling at me?'

'Am I?' He reached for her hand, twining her fingers with his and tugging her gently towards him. He craved the contact even now, felt his heartbeat start to slow as her hip brushed against his leg. 'I suppose it's because I'm thinking how I'd rather be alone with you upstairs than in this stuffy room listening to people witter on.'

Laurel smiled slightly but he saw a flash of something close to hurt in her clear, aquamarine eyes. 'I rather enjoy the wittering, actually.'

Of course she did. And Cristiano felt a pang of shame for dismissing what he knew was an incredibly important topic. Too much of tonight was putting him off balance, out of sorts. And the only way he knew to rectify it was to put things back the way he was used to having them. Laurel in his bed. End of story.

'How about this?' he suggested in a lazy murmur. 'Fifteen more minutes of wittering, we say our goodbyes and then we head upstairs?'

Laurel was eyeing him thoughtfully, in a way Cristiano didn't particularly like. As if she saw through his suggestion to something underneath that he tried to hide, and hell if he even knew what it was.

'We'll miss dinner.'

'I don't care.'

There was a pause as she looked at him, seeming to see far too much. 'All right,' she said softly. 'If that's what you want.'

'It is.' It had to be. And yet, as he watched Laurel begin to make her farewells to the people she'd been talking to, he also felt that it wasn't.

Somehow he wasn't getting what he wanted out of this deal, yet at the same time he was getting far more than he'd ever expected or asked for.

Ten minutes later they were leaving the ballroom. Laurel was silent and pensive as they stepped into the lift and soared up to their private suite, and although he wanted to Cristiano couldn't quite make himself take her in his arms. Turn this into the simple physical exchange he'd told himself he wanted it to be.

What was keeping him from it, damn it? Every nerve felt scraped raw, every sense on high alert as the lifts opened into the suite.

Laurel walked into the suite ahead of him, looking so elegant and lovely, and something in Cristiano broke, the fragments hardening into crystalline points. He took a step towards her and she stilled, perhaps sensing the danger in him. The emotion he couldn't express or suppress, the emotion he couldn't afford to feel.

'Cristiano...?' She turned to him, eyebrows raised in uncertain query.

'Turn around,' Cristiano said, his voice low and hard, a demand that brooked no opposition.

Laurel stared at him for a moment, a faint frown drawing her eyebrows together, and then wordlessly she turned around.

Cristiano stepped towards her and with one swift tug he unzipped her dress.

CHAPTER THIRTEEN

LAUREL FELT THE cool air brush her back and drew in a sharp breath. Cristiano pushed the gown off her shoulders and then slid it down so it pooled about her waist. He didn't speak, and she felt the tension and something inexplicably like anger rolling off him in powerful waves. Felt a tremble of both fear and excitement in herself because, no matter how he treated her, it seemed she couldn't get enough of his touch. But what was going on?

'Cristiano, what—?'

'Don't talk.' He spoke flatly, and Laurel fell silent, even more apprehensive now.

Cristiano stepped behind her, so she felt his powerful frame practically pulsing into hers. He reached up and covered her breasts with his palms, the touch possessive and sure, making her ache. She sagged a little against him as his thumb teased the aching peaks of her breasts and he dropped a kiss onto the curve of her shoulder. And, even though she didn't want to, even though something about this felt completely off, Laurel responded.

A shudder ripped through her as Cristiano rocked against her and her dress slid into a gauzy pool about her feet. She was wearing nothing but a thong—the style of the dress had prohibited a bra—and Cristiano was fully dressed. Fully in control. Everything about this felt unequal. *Wrong*.

'Cristiano…'

'I said, don't talk.' He trailed his hands along her rib cage and then anchored her hips against him. Laurel couldn't keep a moan from escaping her as he pushed against her, and a blaze of pleasure pulsed between her thighs. She threw out a hand towards the hall table to brace herself and Cristiano laughed softly.

'You're not going to fall. Trust me, *bella*.'

She heard the sound of him unzipping his trousers and then taking a condom from his pocket and, with a strength she hadn't expected, she wrenched away, stumbling over her dress before she righted herself. Her breath came in ragged pants as she turned to look at him.

Colour slashed his sharp cheekbones and his eyes glittered with silvery, metallic intent.

'I may be your mistress,' Laurel gasped out, 'but I am not your whore.' And then, not trusting herself to say anything more, she stalked towards the bedroom, slamming the door behind her.

A shudder went through her and Laurel forced herself to blink back tears. What a way to ruin what had been a happy evening. What a way to make her feel excruciatingly cheap. Laurel searched for comfort clothes, but she didn't have any. Sexy nightgowns, provocative lingerie, coordinated outfits, evening gowns. Not a T-shirt or pair of comfy yoga pants to be found.

With a sudden cry she tipped a drawer out and let

the silky garments spill onto the floor. For good measure she kicked them, lobbing them into the corner of the room. She hated everything about her situation here, and even herself, for responding to Cristiano even when he treated her like the trollop he seemed to think she still was.

With another cry she yanked the evening gowns off their padded hangers and threw them in the corner with the rest of the slinky clothes and lingerie.

They might have cost a fortune, but she didn't want them. Didn't want any of it. Ten more days, she told herself. Ten more days and then she never had to see Cristiano again.

Damn it, why did that thought hurt?

A knock sounded on the door. 'Go away,' Laurel called raggedly, the words ripped from her. 'Go *away*, Cristiano.'

She reached for the terrycloth dressing gown hanging on the bathroom door and shrugged into it. Then she pulled the pins from her hair, flinging them on to the dressing table. She'd really been looking forward to tonight. Excited to talk about something that mattered, to feel like more than a mistress. But Cristiano seemed determined to remind her of her lowly status.

Why?

'Laurel,' Cristiano called, his voice low. 'I'm sorry.'

She stilled at the words, which sounded surprisingly heartfelt. She didn't open the door, though.

'Laurel? Did you hear me?'

'Yes. I'm not sure I care, though.' Which was a lie.

'Please open the door.'

'Why? So you can finish what you started? I'm not interested, Cristiano, and, no matter what our *arrange-*

ment, I'm not available on demand.' She choked out the words, hating herself. Hating everything.

'I'm not... I just want to talk. Please.'

Laurel hesitated, then, because she was so angry and she wanted someone to yell at, never mind what Cristiano wanted to say, she stalked to the door and threw it open. 'Fine.'

He turned and walked into the living area and, after a few seconds where she struggled to control her temper and regain her composure, she followed him.

Cristiano stood with his back to her, having shed his tuxedo jacket and bow tie. Laurel tightened the sash on her dressing gown and stiffened her shoulders. 'Well? What did you want to say to me?'

'I am sorry.'

'You said that already.' She was in no mood to be soft and understanding. 'Although I actually question what you're even sorry for. You have the uncanny ability to make me feel cheap without even trying.'

'Actually,' Cristiano said as he turned around, 'I was trying.'

'Oh.' Laurel blinked, absorbing that awful statement. 'Is that somehow supposed to make me feel better?'

'No.' Cristiano rubbed his jaw. He looked haggard suddenly, the stubble glinting on his jaw, his eyes shadowed. Haggard and yet still so impossibly sexy, with a few studs on his tuxedo shirt undone, revealing the lean column of his throat, the bronzed perfection of his chest. But she couldn't think about that now. 'I was just stating a fact,' he said.

'Thanks for that.' She shook her head slowly as tears threatened once again. But, no, she would *not* cry. She wouldn't let Cristiano see how he affected her. Hurt her. And yet she needed to know. 'Why?' she whispered.

Cristiano raked a hand through his close-cropped hair. 'I... I don't know.'

'I was having a good time tonight, you know,' she told him, forcing her voice not to wobble. 'Talking about things that mattered. Feeling important. A small thing, no doubt, and probably pathetic, but it mattered to me. I'm not... I don't want to be your...your sex toy.'

'You're not,' Cristiano insisted in a low voice.

'Your convenient mistress, then. You pulled me from the gala before it had hardly started, and with everyone watching you took me upstairs and treated me like a—like a—' Her voice choked and she struggled to go on.

'Laurel, please. Don't.' Cristiano sounded genuinely anguished. 'I shouldn't have... I'm sorry.'

'So you say. But I still don't understand why you treated me like that.' She drew a shaking breath. 'Do you get your kicks from humiliating women?'

'Of course not.' He sounded angry now, colour slashing his cheekbones. 'I wasn't trying to humiliate you.'

'Just making me feel cheap, then. As usual.'

'Just reminding you of our relationship!' he exploded. 'Reminding myself.' He turned away, raking his hands through his hair again, leaving them on top of his head as he blew out a long, weary breath. 'And you were enjoying it, so don't pretend otherwise.'

'I can't help how I respond to you,' Laurel returned with as much dignity as she could muster. 'I wish I could.'

'Do you?' He let out a humourless laugh.

'*Yes*. I know what you think of me, how little you think of me, and yet I still melt like butter when you so much as crook your finger. That's humiliating.'

'You have no idea what I think of you,' Cristiano said, and dropped his hands.

'Your actions give me a pretty good idea.'

'No.' He turned around to face her. 'Because the truth is I think you're amazing. Smart and driven, kind and compassionate.' Laurel's mouth dropped open as she stared at him in complete shock. 'And that's the reason I took you from the gala, Laurel. That's the reason I brought you up here and tried to remind us both that this is just about sex. Because I'm starting to care about you, and I don't want to.'

He hadn't meant to say all that. And now that he had Cristiano fought the urge to retreat or lash out, either one, something to mitigate the damage he'd just inflicted on himself. Laurel was staring at him, her mouth hanging open, looking completely gobsmacked, and no wonder.

'Wow,' she said finally, and she shook her head. 'Wow. Am I supposed to be touched? *Thankful?*'

The scorn in her voice shocked him. He hadn't been expecting it. He had, he realised, been expecting her to be surprised and moved and—*hell!*—pleased. He'd given her more emotion, more of *himself*, than he had any other woman. Yet Laurel didn't seem to appreciate that fact.

'No,' he said after a moment, his voice stiff. 'Of course not. I was just trying to explain.'

'Trying to explain how you behaved like a complete bastard? Thanks. I feel so much better now.'

He stared at her, anger crystallising inside him. 'Glad to hear it,' he bit out. This is what he got for being honest. He supposed it was better than having her go all dewy-eyed on him, although right now he wouldn't have minded a little softness. Laurel was all hard, glittering edges, filled with a fury he didn't fully understand.

Then, abruptly, she deflated. She walked slowly to an ornate sofa, all gilt curlicues and striped silk, and sank onto it. 'I don't understand you,' she whispered. 'You start to care about me and you treat me even more like you don't?'

Cristiano felt the stirrings of shame and even embarrassment. When she put it like that, it sounded ridiculous and infantile. 'Basically, yes,' he said, and sat opposite her. 'That's what happened.'

'Why?'

Cristiano didn't answer for a long moment. He already felt flayed raw, exposed in a way that made him want to both cringe and attack. 'Remember when you said you didn't want to fall in love with anyone?'

Laurel's eyes widened and Cristiano silently cursed. He had *not* meant to say the dreaded L-word. 'Yes…'

'In a similar way I don't want to care about anyone,' he clarified swiftly. 'Never mind actually fall in love.'

'Because the women you've known, your father's women, were untrustworthy?'

'Yes.' That wasn't the whole truth, but it would suffice for now.

'But you seem to get angry when I show I'm not

like those women,' Laurel pointed out with infuriatingly clear logic. 'When I'm acting differently, like tonight. You got angry because I was talking about nursing, not because I was being as shallow and mercenary as you once assumed me to be.'

'That's not why I got angry.'

'Why, then?'

Cristiano stared at her in frustration, his jaw locked so tightly he felt as if he could break a tooth. This conversation wasn't going anywhere good. Laurel was far too persistent and smart to be fobbed off with some vague half-truths.

'Because you're too good for me,' he said finally, the words ripped from him. 'I want you to be shallow and mercenary, because then this makes sense. A sexual arrangement, nothing more. But when you talk about nursing or your grandfather—or listen to what people say or *laugh*—then it turns into something else, and I don't want that.' He injected a grim note of finality into his voice. 'At all.'

Laurel sat back against the sofa, looking a little winded. Then she straightened and said, 'I didn't ask you to want it.'

'I know,' Cristiano said shortly. He hardly needed the reminder, and it rubbed raw, especially now.

'But,' Laurel continued slowly, 'Is it such a bad thing—to care about someone? Because if I'm not like those other women…your father's…then what's the problem? The risk?'

And just like that she got to the painful, beating heart of it and Cristiano had no idea how to answer. So he told her the truth. 'This isn't about me thinking you're like them,' he said. 'It's about losing control.'

Laurel's eyebrows rose. 'Losing control? How?'

Cristiano shifted restlessly in his seat and then in one abrupt movement he rose from the sofa and paced the spacious room, feeling caged by his memories.

'Any serious relationship—a loving marriage, anything—involves a loss of control. A giving up. And that's something I can't stand. And, yes—' he cut across her before she could say anything '—it's because of my childhood. We're all products of our growing up; you were right there. But it's not because of my father's mistresses, or his second wife, or your mother. It's because of mine.'

The silence between them felt both heavy and taut. Laurel was gazing at him steadily, a softness to her expression that made him want to bury himself in her arms. Seek comfort when he had given her none.

'What about your mother?' she asked when the silence had stretched to snapping point.

'She loved my father. And he loved her.' Cristiano felt his throat working as he swallowed hard. 'Very much.'

'Was that such a bad thing?' Laurel asked softly.

'Yes, because their love was…turbulent. Passionate. They were always fighting and falling back in love— throwing vases, breaking plates, what have you.'

'Not every loving marriage is like that.'

'No, but the loss of control is still there. Being enslaved to your emotions and at the mercy of another person.'

'A person you trust.'

'Maybe.' Cristiano continued pacing, his head down, teeth gritted. 'But maybe you shouldn't trust anyone that much.'

'What happened to your mother, Cristiano?' The question was soft and sad, so full of compassion, that it nearly broke him.

'She and my father had an almighty row. I think they enjoyed arguing, the intensity of it, and of course the passionate making up. This time she flounced out of the house. She'd done it before; I remember watching from the window as she'd speed down the driveway in her little red convertible. I never knew if she was going to come back or not.' The memories were hitting him now, wave after relentless wave, reminding him of the turmoil and tumult of his childhood. The arguments, the shrieking voices, the feeling, as a boy, that he never knew what to expect. Who to trust. Or what it meant truly to love someone.

'That must have been very hard on you,' Laurel said quietly. Her eyes were filled with a sorrowful compassion that Cristiano feared would be his undoing. Perhaps her fury and scorn would have been better to deal with. He could have matched them. But this…

'There's no shame in it, you know,' she said. 'In feeling hurt.'

Oh, but there was. Because it revealed a weakness in him, a gaping, bleeding need that felt like the very life were draining out of him.

'Anyway,' he resumed after a moment, when he trusted himself to speak normally, 'that time, that argument, she left in her convertible and she didn't come back. She died,' he explained succinctly. 'Crashed her car straight into a tree.'

'Oh, Cristiano…'

'The thing is,' he continued, determined to say it all now. 'It was a straight, flat road. No other cars were involved. And the tree was about ten feet away from the road. So why did she crash? How?'

Laurel's face paled, her eyes wide and dark. 'You mean you think she did it on purpose?'

'It seems likely, doesn't it?'

'I don't know...'

'That's what love does to you,' he finished flatly. 'It kills you.' When he said the words out loud they sounded melodramatic, even childish, yet he knew he meant them. Utterly.

'Oh, Cristiano.' Laurel's face was suffused with sadness. 'It doesn't have to. I have to believe that.' She let out a sad little laugh. 'Not that I would really know.'

'What do you mean?'

'The people I've loved have always left. My father, my mother, your father.' She gave him an almost apologetic look. 'You might not want to hear that, but I loved him. He was like a father to me for those three years—showing up to school concerts, taking me for a ride in his fancy car. The only father I've ever really had, my mother's parade of boyfriends aside.'

'I... I didn't realise.' He hadn't given Laurel's feelings so much as a thought when he'd told his father about Elizabeth's secret bank account—and she'd only been fourteen. How could he have been so thoughtless? So selfish? Yes, Elizabeth had been a thief. But Laurel had been collateral damage, and he hadn't even cared. 'I'm sorry.'

'It was a long time ago. I didn't say all that to make you feel sorry for me. I just wanted to say that I understand, at least a little bit. But I guess I'm still hoping that it can be different for me some day, with someone new. They won't leave.' Her lips trembled and she forced them into a smile. 'They won't want to leave.'

'Laurel…'

'And it can be different for you, Cristiano, one day. One day maybe you won't believe that love kills or even hurts. You'll see that it can heal and restore and strengthen.'

'You have a lot of faith,' Cristiano said in a low voice. He was unbearably moved by her hope, when she had so little to hope for. So many people had left her.

'Not really,' Laurel admitted with a shaky laugh. 'I talk a big game.'

Cristiano nodded slowly. He felt weary and aching, yet, strangely, cautiously hopeful—although about what, he couldn't quite say. Wasn't willing to verbalise.

'Thank you,' he said after a moment. 'For listening. For understanding. And I am sorry for…before.' He paused, weighing his words, his feelings. Truth versus safety. Caring versus control. 'The question is,' he said slowly, 'what do we do now?'

CHAPTER FOURTEEN

LAUREL SHIFTED WHERE she stood, trying to ease the ache in her feet. Stilettos were not for the faint of heart, and she'd worn them five days running. For the last week she and Cristiano had been touring his hotels across Europe—first Paris, then London, Milan and now Barcelona. He'd been checking on his managers, doing business, and she'd been enjoying seeing places in Europe she'd never thought she'd have the opportunity to see.

Ever since their surprisingly honest conversation after the charity gala, things had shifted between them. They weren't in love, and Laurel knew better than to start painting rainbows in the sky or building fairy-tale castles. She didn't even want to, because she knew dreaming of a happy ending with Cristiano was foolish to the extreme. But she'd started to relax and enjoy their time together, and he had as well.

They'd chatted, laughed, teased and talked. And made love. Sex was no longer a transaction, but a sharing, an expression…but of what? That was a question Laurel didn't let herself ask, much less answer.

They might have made some much-needed strides in their love affair, but Cristiano was still a man who guarded his back and his heart. Trust didn't come easily, and love didn't come at all. But at least Laurel was going in with her eyes wide open; she had no intention of falling in love with Cristiano Ferrero. The trouble was, he was starting to make that rather difficult.

'Just another few minutes,' he murmured as he came to her side at the cocktail party they were attending— yet another social occasion that doubled as networking for Cristiano. 'You look like your feet are killing you.'

'They are,' Laurel admitted. 'I'm not used to wearing high heels this much. For work, it's usually sensible lace-ups.'

'I'll give you a foot-rub later,' Cristiano promised, and her stomach swirled with pleasure and pure, simple happiness. Yes, Cristiano was giving her far too many reasons to fall in love with him.

They made their farewells a few minutes later and stepped outside into a balmy Spanish night, the scent of orange blossom on the evening air.

A limo was waiting for them, as it always was, and Laurel slid into the sumptuous leather interior with a contented sigh. A week of this and she'd become accustomed to luxury.

Cristiano settled in next to her and reached for her leg, lifting her foot onto his lap. He slipped off her stiletto with a wince.

'You could kill someone with one of these things.'

Laurel leaned her head back against the seat, revelling in the feel of his powerful thumbs rotating circles on the balls of her feet. 'I practically did. I embedded one in Rico Bavasso's palm.'

'Did you?' Cristiano let out an admiring laugh.

'Served him right. No wonder he was rather put out, though.'

'Do you think he's really got the message?' Laurel asked, even though the last thing she wanted to talk about was Rico Bavasso.

'Undoubtedly. He's attached himself to a French singer—some wannabe pop star.'

'He has? That was quick.' She frowned. 'Although I don't particularly like the thought of him inflicting himself on some other woman. Do you think…is he really dangerous?'

'He attacked you, didn't he?' Cristiano's thumbs paused on the balls of her feet. 'But I might have exaggerated his need for revenge.'

She nearly jerked her foot out of his grasp. 'What?'

'I had some real concern, but…' Cristiano's smile was unrepentant. 'I wanted to keep you to myself for a little longer, and Bavasso provided a convenient excuse.'

She laughed, relaxing against the seat. A few days ago she would have been outraged by his confession. Now, in the security of their relationship—and, yes, she used that word with care—she only felt amused. 'I'm glad to know that now.' Cristiano continued his massage and Laurel let out a groan of pleasure.

'I will never wear heels like these again, ever.'

'What about the event in Madrid tomorrow?'

'There's another event?' She couldn't keep the disappointment out of her voice. The last week had been a lovely whirlwind, but she was *tired*.

Cristiano looked surprised. 'Are you telling me you don't like parties?'

'I'm getting weary of them,' Laurel admitted. 'Tiring of being "on" all the time, getting dressed up, and the hair and make-up and the posing…' She sighed. 'I just want a return to some kind of normality. To be able to relax and be myself.' *With you.* Admitting that might be a step too far.

Cristiano slid his hand from her foot to her calf, trailing his fingers along her skin meaningfully. 'I can think of a way to relax.'

'I'm sure you can.' Laurel's breath hitched as he smoothed his hand from her knee to her hip. Over a week and she still hadn't tired of his touch, not remotely. A single fingertip trailed along her skin and, yes, she still melted. Just like butter.

'Perhaps we could go somewhere quieter,' Cristiano said, his hand sliding up and down her leg. 'Somewhere…relaxing.'

'You know,' Laurel murmured, watching his hand move up and down, 'you can make anything sound like an innuendo.'

'It's a gift.'

'It must be.'

The limo pulled up in front of their hotel and Cristiano helped her out. Laurel's body tingled with anticipation. Every night this week they'd left a party and gone to Cristiano's private suite. Every night he'd taken her in his arms, taken her to bed, and she still felt the fizz of excitement, the sizzle of desire.

They rode the lift in silence, and then when the doors opened Cristiano turned to her, as he always did. His teeth gleamed in the darkness.

'Come here,' he whispered, and Laurel came willingly. Eagerly.

* * *

She woke up the next morning tangled in navy satin sheets, sunlight spilling through the floor-to-ceiling windows, a sleepy smile on her face. Cristiano was gone, but he usually rose early to work on his laptop, then woke her up by bringing her coffee and croissants. More than once they'd made love amongst the crumbs.

Now he appeared in the doorway, freshly showered and shaven, wearing a pair of charcoal trousers and an open-necked button-down shirt in deep blue. As always, he possessed the power to steal her breath.

'Good morning.' He handed her a steaming mug of coffee which Laurel accepted gratefully. 'I thought we'd do something different today.'

'Oh?' She took a sip, her eyebrows raised in expectation.

Cristiano braced one shoulder against the doorframe. 'You said you were tired of the social whirl, and I think we could both use a break.' He paused, his gaze resting thoughtfully on her. 'So I thought we could go to Capri.'

'Capri?'

'Yes, the island in the Bay of Naples—do you know it?'

'I've heard of it, but I've never been there.'

'It's a lovely place. We can take a short flight to Naples and then a ferry to the island.' He paused, and Laurel tensed, for she could tell there was something more he was going to say. Something important. 'It's where my father lives.'

Her eyes widened as realisation shot through her. 'Your father…? You mean we're going to—to visit him?' She could hardly believe it. Cristiano rarely talked about his father, and when he did it was with reluctance, and perhaps even disdain. Their relationship hadn't been close ten years ago, and it didn't appear to be any closer now.

And yet...

'Yes, I thought you might like to see him.' Cristiano took a sip of coffee, his gaze on the windows and the view of the city stretched out before them. 'Since you seemed close to him all those years ago.'

'I was.' She swallowed, nerves fluttering in her middle. 'But I don't actually know if he'd like to see me.' Lorenzo had sent her and Elizabeth away without so much as a backward glance. Even now, the memory had the power to sting and wound.

'I've already called him,' Cristiano answered, moving his gaze back to her. 'And he does.'

Cristiano watched as Laurel's lips parted and tears filled her eyes. 'Oh...he does?' She sniffed. 'That's... Well, that's wonderful. Thank you, Cristiano.'

He nodded, not trusting himself to say more. He still wasn't comfortable with this kind of emotion, but he was trying to get used to it. For the last week he'd been living in a limbo of deep enjoyment and relentless discomfort, pain and pleasure mixed. Because being intimate with someone—physically, emotionally—was a whole new realm of experience, and one he wasn't entirely sure about. The vulnerability, the intensity, the *risk*. And yet the more time he spent with Laurel, the more he wanted to.

He also wanted to make amends as best as he could. More and more over the last week he'd realised what a disservice he'd done Laurel when he'd told his father about her mother's bank account. Yes, Elizabeth was a gold-digging schemer and a thief, but that hadn't been Laurel's fault, and she'd suffered as a result. If he'd handled the situation differently, if he hadn't been determined to paint the grimmest picture to his father, maybe things would have worked out differently. At least perhaps Lorenzo would have stayed in touch with his stepdaughter.

'I can't believe it,' Laurel said as she hugged her knees, her golden-brown curls tumbling about her shoulders. 'To see him again... Are you sure he wants to see me?' She glanced at him, eyes full of apprehension as she nibbled her lower lip.

Guilt pierced Cristiano with poison-tipped arrows. He hadn't told Laurel the extent of his involvement in their parents' divorce. At first it hadn't seemed relevant and now he knew it would hurt her and, more alarmingly, jeopardise their fledgling relationship. Because he was already thinking about ways to keep her around after the two weeks were up...assuming she wasn't pregnant. Sometimes he found himself half-hoping she was.

'I'm sure,' he said firmly. 'He was thrilled to hear we'd been in contact.'

Laurel raised her eyebrows. 'Does he...does he know how much contact we've been in?'

Cristiano smiled. 'I didn't give him details, but I think he guesses.' He paused. 'Is that a bad thing?'

'No. I just...' She hunched her shoulders, her gaze sliding away. 'We've less than a week left,' she said quietly, and Cristiano felt as if the breath had been punched from his lungs.

'What does that matter?' he asked when he trusted himself to speak normally. To sound unconcerned.

'I don't want your father to get his hopes up,' Laurel explained. 'To think something more might be going on.' She gave him a direct look, her chin slightly lifted, showing courage and determination and a hint of vulnerability.

'Don't worry,' he said, wondering how he was meant to reassure her. Should he tell her his father wouldn't get his hopes up, or that perhaps he should? When, if ever, should he tell her he wanted more from this relationship than another week?

The question, of course, was how much more. Cristiano had tried to envision different scenarios in his head, and most of them involved Laurel being his permanent, full-time mistress. He wasn't ready to countenance anything more, yet he knew instinctively she'd resist such a role. So he waited, saying nothing, hoping things would be clarified for both of them in time.

'We should get going,' he said as he turned from the room. 'Our plane leaves in a few hours.'

A short while later they were leaving the suite for the airport. Laurel was dressed in a cheerful polka-dot sundress—after she'd thrown all the clothes Cristiano had given her onto the floor, he'd offered to buy her new ones. She'd happily gone out to far more modest shops and picked up a couple of casual outfits. She'd insisted on paying for them herself, but Cristiano had insisted more, and eventually she'd acquiesced.

As the limo took them to the airport she gazed at him speculatively. 'When was the last time you saw your father?'

Cristiano shrugged. 'A year or so.'

'You don't see him very often.'

Another shrug; her perception still possessed the power to rub him raw. 'I'm very busy.'

'But you're not close,' Laurel persisted quietly, and Cristiano sighed.

'No,' he agreed, 'I suppose we aren't.'

'Why not?'

Cristiano gazed out at the blur of buildings streaming by. 'Because I don't respect him,' he said at last. 'And it's difficult to have a relationship, at least a positive one, when there is no respect involved.'

Laurel considered this for a moment. 'Does he respect you?'

'I have no idea, and I really don't much care.'

'Why don't you respect him?' She was like a dog with a bone, worrying away at it, getting to the bloody marrow.

'Do we really have to talk about this?'

'We're about to go visit him, so yes, I think we do. Why don't you, Cristiano?' She asked the question softly, her voice filled with compassion. She was ready to understand him, and it made him answer reluctantly.

'Because he's thrown his life away on love.'

'Ah.' She nodded thoughtfully, not looking as disappointed in his answer as he'd expected, and perversely wanted her to be. 'So you're angry at him for wasting his life.'

When she put it like that... 'I'm not angry,' he said tersely. 'Not exactly.' Except, he realised as he said it, it wasn't true. He *was* angry, but it seemed childish somehow. An emotion he wanted to rise above.

'It must not have been easy,' Laurel said quietly,

'to lose your mother the way you did. And then to see your father fall in love with women who weren't in love with him.'

'Do you count your mother in that number?' Cristiano asked more sharply than he intended but, damn it, he felt so raw.

'No,' Laurel said softly. 'I don't. But I understand why you would.' She reached for his hand and Cristiano threaded his fingers through hers, taking a deep breath to compose himself. These honest, emotional conversations still felt new and difficult. Painful. But he was trying, because he knew Laurel wanted more from him, and amazingly, alarmingly, he wanted it too. He was tired of the superficial, sex-only arrangements he'd had before.

And yet that question niggled at his mind—*how much more do you want?*

The rest of the journey to Capri passed pleasantly enough; Laurel stood at the railing of the ferry and gazed out at the blue-green sea, jewel-bright under the afternoon sun.

'It's so lovely,' she murmured. 'I'd forgotten how lovely it was in Italy.' She tilted her face to the sun, her whole body seeming to drink in the light. If Cristiano could have painted her like that, he would have. She was the essence of happiness, of joy and freedom, a faint smile curving her lovely mouth, her hair blowing in the wind.

They walked from the ferry landing to the funicular, the cable railway that went to the town centre. From the *piazzetta* they walked to Lorenzo's villa, which was on the outskirts of the town. Laurel gazed round at the white villas with their brightly painted shutters and pots of trailing bougainvillea, delighting in everything.

And then they were there, standing in front of the steep, winding steps that led to his father's villa, a tall, white building near Capri's old town, its terracotta roof tiles blazing under the late-afternoon sun.

Laurel paused, nervousness flitting across her features as she gazed up at the steps, and then shot Cristiano an anxious look.

'Do you really think…?'

'I know,' Cristiano said, and took her hand. They climbed the steps together, then stepped into the airy, sunlit foyer. A housekeeper bustled in with a cheery stream of Italian…and then there he was, Cristiano's father, standing in the doorway, looking older and frailer in the year since he'd last seen him, but also far happier, his face wreathed in smiles as he held his arms out to Laurel.

'*Cara,*' he said in a voice full of welcome and warmth, and with a little stifled cry Laurel ran into his arms.

CHAPTER FIFTEEN

LAUREL STRETCHED OUT on the sun lounger, her heart brimming with happiness. It had been three days since they'd arrived in Capri, and they'd been the best three days of her life.

Seeing Lorenzo again…having him welcome her with open arms and tears in his eyes… Laurel hadn't even realised just how much she'd missed him, the gaping absence he'd left in her life, until she'd ran into his arms and he'd whispered how sorry he was ever to have let her go.

Being with Cristiano out of the public eye, with no fanfare or spectacle, no socialising or small talk, was another wonderful blessing. Finally they could simply *be* with each other, enjoying lazy mornings and lovely, long nights, strolls around Capri and afternoons lounging by the pool. Laurel knew it couldn't last—in just three more days the requisite two weeks would have passed since that first, fateful night. Three more days and she could take a pregnancy test.

And what if she *was* pregnant?

It was a question she hadn't let herself think too much about. In those first difficult days she hadn't wanted to think about it. Hadn't possessed the strength to imagine that dreaded *what if?* scenario.

Now…now she dared not think about it for an entirely different reason. Because part of her, an increasingly large part, was hoping she was pregnant with Cristiano's child.

Logically she knew she probably wasn't pregnant. She was fairly regular and her period wasn't due for at least another week. And in any case she knew a pregnancy wasn't a good idea. She wanted Cristiano to choose to be with her for her own sake, not just to provide for their child. And yet…she wanted Cristiano to choose to be with her.

That was the truth she had to force herself to face, the reality that crowded in during quiet moments. They most likely had only a handful of days left together, yet in the quiet of her mind she dreamed of for ever.

'You look deep in thought.' Lorenzo walked slowly towards the lounger next to Laurel's and sat down carefully. Laurel had noticed, over the last few days, how slowly he moved, how cautiously, and it made her wonder. Worry.

'Not too deep,' she said with a smile and then leaned her head against the lounger. 'It's too beautiful a day for deep thoughts.' The infinity pool shimmered in front of them, surrounded by orange and lemon trees, the roofs of Capri and the sparkling sea in the distance.

'Yes, perhaps it is.' Lorenzo settled himself against his lounger with a slight wince, causing Laurel another pang of worry. 'And where is my son this morning?'

'Catching up on some work, but he promised to join us for lunch.'

'I've never seen him look so happy,' Lorenzo said quietly. 'Thank you.'

Laurel smiled wryly. 'I don't know if it's my doing.'

'Oh, it is, Laurel, I'm sure of it. He's in love with you, even if he doesn't want to realise it.'

She let out a laugh at the older man's perception, hope struggling with fear inside her, a torment of emotion. 'That's the nub of it, isn't it?' she asked, trying to sound light. 'He doesn't want to.'

'Cristiano has always had a deep suspicion of any emotion, particularly love.'

'Yes.' She took a deep breath and let it out slowly. 'He told me a little bit about you and his mother. How much you loved each other.'

'Did he?' Lorenzo nodded slowly. 'Of course, he is only remembering it as a child.'

'Was it different than he said?'

'I don't know what he said, but I can imagine.' Lorenzo sighed, his face looking pale and drawn and old. Again Laurel felt that pang of worry assail her. Lorenzo did not seem a well man. 'My marriage to Gabriella was tempestuous, to say the least,' he continued. 'She thrived on it, all the passion and anger and energy. It made her feel alive, but it drained me.'

'That doesn't sound entirely healthy,' Laurel ventured cautiously.

'No, it wasn't. It was exhausting at the best of times, and incredibly dispiriting at the worst. When she died...' Pain flashed across his face and then was gone. 'I blamed myself. I shouldn't have let her run out the way she did. I knew she was in a temper, and the maddening thing now is I can't even remember what we argued about. That feels wrong, don't you think— to die for something that you've forgotten about? And yet she was in such a rage at the time.'

'That doesn't seem like it was your fault.'

'Perhaps.' Lorenzo was silent for a moment. 'Still I regret it. I regret many things.' He squinted at the horizon, sunlight sparkling off the sea. 'I fear Cristiano is the way he is because of me.'

Laurel knew it to be true, by Cristiano's own admission, but she was interested in Lorenzo's perspective. 'What do you mean, the way he is?'

Lorenzo shrugged. 'What I said before. His deep suspicion of emotion, of love. His determination to be an island, which no man is.' He gave her a small, wistful smile. 'While I am quite the opposite, always searching for something more. The one person who will make me feel connected and whole. I thought I'd found it with your mother.'

Emotion clogged in Laurel's throat. 'She thought she'd found it with you.'

'Did she?'

Laurel forced the words past the lump in her throat. 'I know she stole from you, Lorenzo, but it wasn't… She didn't…'

'In the years since,' Lorenzo said slowly, 'I've thought often about the money your mother took. Money I would have given her freely, but I wonder if she knew that.'

'She lived in fear of being poor,' Laurel said quietly. 'Poor and abandoned. She always has.'

'In any case, I regret sending you both away so precipitously, without so much as a discussion.' Lorenzo shook his head sorrowfully. 'I have regretted it for a long time, especially how you, one so young, must have felt.'

Laurel blinked hard. 'It was…difficult,' she admitted, and Lorenzo's face crumpled a bit.

'I'm so sorry, my dear. I felt so betrayed, you see, because of the experience with my second wife. Did Cristiano tell you about that?'

'Yes, a little.'

'He convinced me that Elizabeth would leave, and in my weakness and self-doubt I believed him. She was so lovely and vibrant and young. I often wondered how she could possibly love me—me, and not just my money.' He shook his head, sadness creasing the already deep lines of his face.

'I suppose it's a problem any rich man faces,' Laurel said carefully. 'And I am not blind to my mother's faults, Lorenzo. She had a hard childhood and money is important to her. She's become used to a certain standard, and she'd lived her life to make sure she has it.'

Lorenzo smiled. 'I am well aware of Elizabeth's faults as well, my dear. But we all have them, don't we? No one is perfect.'

'No.' And her mother was far from it. Even now Laurel wondered why she defended her. Her mother had used her to win favour with Rico Bavasso, whether she'd meant things to go as far as they had or not. That was kind of hard to forgive, yet Laurel still wanted to forgive her. But that, she realised, was the stark difference between her and Cristiano—despite the mistakes and sorrows of the past, she strove to find forgiveness, redemption, hope. She wanted to believe in love, craved to know it was possible. Cristiano didn't.

Sighing, she settled back against the lounger, her heart twisting inside her. She was falling in love with Cristiano, with his kindness, honesty and sudden, surprising tenderness. The sensitive soul that hid beneath his hardened exterior. She was falling in love with him, but she knew it wasn't a good idea. It would only end in tears. Hers.

Lorenzo reached over and touched her hand. 'Give it time,' he said quietly. 'Give him time. He does love you, you know. He just has to stop fighting it.'

Laurel gazed down at Lorenzo's veined, arthritic hand and blinked back tears. 'Thank you,' she whispered. 'I hope you're right.' It was the closest she'd come to admitting she loved Cristiano.

Lorenzo smiled and removed his hand. 'Living without love is such a waste. Cristiano will realise that in time. And time is something both of you have.'

Laurel couldn't ignore the wistful note of sorrow in Lorenzo's voice. 'Lorenzo,' she said carefully. 'Do you know I work as a nurse? In palliative care?'

He didn't pretend to misunderstand what she was getting at. 'Ah.' He leaned his head back against the lounger and closed his eyes. 'I see.'

'How long have you been ill?' Laurel asked softly.

Lorenzo didn't speak for a long moment. Laurel waited, hoping even now that he might dismiss her concern, tell her he was just an old man who became tired. But, no. He opened his eyes and gazed out at the horizon, lemon-yellow sun and bright blue sky. 'I was diagnosed with cancer of the kidney three months ago. It had spread to my stomach and lungs. There's no stopping it.'

'Oh, Lorenzo.' Laurel gazed at him in deep sadness and sympathy. To have found each other again only for him to be taken away... 'How long?' she asked.

Lorenzo gave a little shrug. 'The doctors do not like to discuss dates. I refused treatment...there was no point, and I do not wish to spend my last days in a hospital, on machines and in great pain.' He sighed. 'A few months, they said, maybe more, maybe less. A year at the most. I have medication for the pain.'

'It doesn't seem like enough. I've noticed you wincing.'

He shrugged again, and Laurel pressed her lips together. 'Pain management is a very important part of end-of-life care, Lorenzo,' she said gently. 'You want your last days to be as pleasant and pain-free as possible, and research shows that you do better physically as well as emotionally if your body doesn't tire itself fighting the pain all the time.'

'Thank you for the advice.' He smiled and touched her hand. 'The medication makes me feel loopy. I don't want to take too much of it.'

'I understand.' And she did, all too well. She dealt with her patients' concerns about the effect of pain relief on their quality of life all the time, and the most important part of palliative care, in her opinion, was letting patients make their own choices for as long as they could. 'Does Cristiano know?' she asked after a moment. Her throat still felt thick and tears crowded at the backs of her eyes. For Lorenzo's sake she didn't want to give in to her own emotion, but she felt unbearably sad at the thought of losing him all over again. And what about Cristiano?

'No,' Lorenzo said after a pause, which was no surprise to Laurel.

'Why haven't you told him?'

Lorenzo shrugged. 'I suppose I wanted to spare him the pain when there is nothing he can do. Cristiano has never been one to accept inaction.'

'True.' Laurel managed a small smile. 'But I think he would want to know.'

'Yes and, now that you are both here, I will tell him. At least he will have you to comfort him, *cara*.' Lorenzo gently touched her cheek, and Laurel smiled through her tears.

Cristiano gazed out at the bright-blue sky and golden sunshine and clenched his jaw so hard it felt as if he might break a tooth. Anger was a far better emotion to feel than grief.

'How long have you known?' he asked.

From behind him Lorenzo stirred and sighed. 'A few months.'

'And you didn't feel the need to tell me?'

'There's nothing you can do, Cristiano.'

'Even so.'

'I suppose I wanted to wait until we were face to face.'

'I would have come sooner if I knew it was important.'

Lorenzo sighed again, the sound soft and sad. 'Would you have?' he asked quietly.

Cristiano turned around, his fists clenched, his heart racing, as if he was preparing for a fight. Spoiling for one, maybe, but he didn't want to antagonise his father now, not when he was so ill. But he didn't know how to be, how to feel. The natural emotion— grief in all of its dark, unrelenting mess—was anathema to him.

'Of course I would have,' he said, but even as the words left his mouth he wondered. Doubted. He'd avoided his father for years, ignored the ways Lorenzo had reached out. Why? Because of his contempt for his father's choices, or for a deeper, more revealing reason?

Because loving someone always hurt.

'Well, I am not quite at my end yet,' Lorenzo said lightly. 'There is time, Cristiano. Time, perhaps, for us to heal old wounds.'

'What old wounds?' Cristiano tried to sound dismissive but the words stuck in his throat like shards of broken glass, and his voice came out sounding strangled.

'I know you harbour anger towards me for my choices.' Lorenzo took a deep, steadying breath. 'In my search for love I let a lot of women into your life. A lot of uncertainty and confusion.'

'I'm a grown man,' Cristiano dismissed. 'And in any case, I survived.'

'But we all want more out of life than survival, don't we? And I fear you have sworn off love because of my experiences.'

Cristiano just shrugged. He didn't trust himself to speak. He didn't know what he'd say, in any case. Yes, he'd sworn off love, and for good reason. And, although the last week and a half had been the best of his life, he still wasn't ready to make that kind of commitment to Laurel. Couldn't open himself up to all the risk and pain. Did that make him an emotional coward? Maybe. But at least he stayed strong. Solitary.

He left his father a short while later, because Lorenzo was clearly tiring, and went in search of Laurel. Twilight was settling over the terrace, the air holding a hint of coolness, as Cristiano stepped outside. Laurel was standing by the balcony, her hands resting on the ornate stone railing, her face tilted to the last dying rays of the sun.

'You spoke to your father?' she asked softly.

'You knew.'

'I guessed.' She turned to him, a world of sorrow in her eyes. 'I spend all my time with people who are dealing with terminal illness. You get to know the signs.'

'I wish he'd told me.'

'I know.' She moved towards him, all fluid grace, and put her arms around him. For a second Cristiano resisted. Part of him wanted to stay strong, separate. But the pain he felt was too much for him to bear on his own, and the sweet, pliant warmth of her body was the balm he so desperately needed.

He pulled her close, burying his face in her fragrant hair. 'I've always tried to live my life so I have no regrets,' he muttered against her hair, his eyes clenched shut. 'I thought that was the best way to be, and yet now I feel awash with regret. Too many things to feel sorry for. To atone for.'

'Regret isn't a bad thing, Cristiano,' Laurel said gently. 'It doesn't have to be about guilt or shame. It's a strong and brave thing to feel, because it allows you to take responsibility for your actions and make a positive choice for the future.'

'That sounds very wise.'

'I've talked a lot to people who are dealing with regrets. It's something you think about as your life comes to an end. And,' she added, a tremor in her voice, 'I've had regrets of my own.'

He eased back, searching her face. 'What do you regret?'

'Letting my mother talk me into coming to meet Rico Bavasso, for one.'

'But, if you hadn't, you would never have met me again.'

She smiled, but it wavered on her face, as uncertain as a shadow slipping away. 'You don't regret meeting me, do you, Laurel?' Cristiano asked with more urgency than he meant to reveal or even feel. 'Do you?'

'No.' Still she sounded uncertain, and that hurt him more than he expected.

'Why? Why would you?' Of course he knew the reasons, yet still he asked. Torturing himself because he couldn't help it.

'It's not as if this is going to last,' Laurel said after a moment, her voice so quiet Cristiano strained to hear it, even though he was standing right next to her. 'You don't have a monopoly on pain, Cristiano.' She spoke without rancour, merely stating truth. 'I don't want to get hurt, either.'

'I don't want to hurt you.' He meant it more than he'd ever thought possible.

She gave him a sad, wistful smile. 'Sometimes we don't have a choice in these things.'

'But if you're pregnant…' It was a possibility he'd

considered unfortunate mere days ago, but now it opened up a whole new realm of choice to him. To them. 'If you're pregnant, I will marry you.' He didn't know whether it was a threat or promise. Both, perhaps.

'And if I'm not?' She gazed up at him, her face cast in silvery light from the rising moon, her eyes large and clear, hiding nothing. The choice was his, to stay or to go, to risk or to hide. To love or to leave.

Cristiano's mind spun. He thought of his father wasting away in bed, alone after so many years and still heartbroken. His mother, storming out in a fearsome rage, only to go to her death, and for what? *For what?* 'We don't have to make any decisions right away,' he said, and disappointment flickered across Laurel's face before she nodded.

'No,' she agreed. 'I suppose not.'

It wasn't the answer she'd hoped to hear, that much was obvious, and Cristiano could hardly blame her. Who wanted prevarications at a moment like this? She wanted him to sweep her up into his arms, kiss her and tell her he loved her. He couldn't do that, but two out of three wasn't bad, was it? It was all he had to offer. All he had to give.

He pulled her closer and pressed a kiss to her forehead, then to her lips. Gentle kisses that were meant as promises, although of what he could not say.

And Laurel accepted them, her arms coming around him, her soft, warm body fitting to his. Desire flared inside him, along with something stronger—a soul-deep craving to connect in this moment, not to feel alone. Not to be solitary, even if that meant admitting weakness. In this moment he needed it. He deepened the kiss, driving his hands through her hair, searching for her and branding her. Seeking solace as much as satisfaction, and finding both in this. In them.

Laurel answered him kiss for kiss, their breathing turning harsh and ragged, their bodies coming together in a connection so piercing and deep it felt exquisitely painful. She didn't protest when he held her by the hips and hoisted her up onto the balcony railing. She wrapped her legs around his waist as he stroked her, finding her ready for him.

It was a matter of mere moments as he slid the condom from his pocket, fumbling with it in his haste, then thrust into her, the sense of completeness, of rightness, overwhelming him so that tears came to his eyes.

Laurel arched closer, drawing him in further, matching every thrust as they both found their release.

Cristiano cried out, the sound splintering the still night air, his heart thudding against Laurel's as he rested his forehead against her and drew shuddering breaths.

His body felt sated, drugged with the aftermath of pleasure, yet something deep inside him still ached and yearned. This, which had always been enough, wasn't any longer.

CHAPTER SIXTEEN

HOLDING ON TO happiness felt like trying to cup water in your hands. No matter how you tried, it still trickled out. Two days passed, lovely, golden days, yet they possessed an urgency, a fear, that they hadn't before. Laurel felt it in herself, and she also felt it in Cristiano. Time was running out.

And, even though it didn't have to be this way, even though Laurel knew if Cristiano asked her she would stay, she would try, she would risk it all, she knew in her bones, in her very soul, that he wasn't going to ask.

He thought about it. She saw it in his eyes—the faraway look that came over him, followed by a hardening of his features into an unwelcome resolve she wanted to scream and fight against. She wanted to rail and weep—to demand why he thought staying safe was so important, why he didn't think risking life and love with her was worth it—but she didn't because, when it came down to it, she was afraid too.

The possibility of a face-to-face, outright rejection from Cristiano, of pushing for answers and then getting ones she didn't want, kept her silent. She didn't care about her dignity or her pride, but she didn't think her heart could take one of his crushing set-downs. Not after all they'd shared.

As for the possibility of pregnancy… With every passing day Laurel wondered and hoped, even though logic told her it was unlikely. And yet…as a nurse she knew it wasn't out of the question that she might have fallen pregnant on that first night, no matter how she'd once scoffed at such a notion.

It still seemed crazy to hope for such a thing, yet she feared it was the only way Cristiano would commit to her. She could hardly believe she'd fallen into that age-old trap of wanting a baby to snare a man. Was she that weak? That desperate?

Twelve days after Laurel had first stumbled into Cristiano's penthouse, she lay in his bed, her head resting on his shoulder, her fingers trailing a light path down his muscled chest. She didn't think she'd ever get tired of touching him. She'd spent a good part of the last two weeks touching him, smoothing the satiny, muscled perfection of him, learning the planes and angles of his well-defined body.

And yet so much more than that too… With a pang she thought of the laughter they'd shared, the surprising conversations, the simple pleasure of being in his company. Yet the next two days pressed down on her, an unbearable weight. Was it really going to end so soon?

'The day after tomorrow it will have been two weeks,' she said softly, because she couldn't not say it. Underneath her hand she felt Cristiano tense.

'So it will.' An answer that gave nothing away, of course. He never did, especially in moments like these.

She recalled that deceptively mild tone from their first days together and feared its return.

'Shall I take a pregnancy test, then?' she asked.

'That was always the plan.' Just in case she'd needed the reminder, which she didn't. He paused, his body still tense next to hers. 'Do you think there's a possibility...?'

'I don't know.' But she hoped. She'd taken to wondering if the slightest queasiness, the faint cramping, meant anything. Stupid, she knew, because even if she was pregnant it was too early for noticeable symptoms. Yet, just like with her mother, with everything in her life, she hoped for the best. She wanted to believe that she and Cristiano could be together—but did it really have to take a pregnancy to make it happen? It seemed her hope didn't stretch to Cristiano himself, to him changing and learning to love her, being willing to make that jump and take that risk.

'We'll find out soon enough,' he said, his tone repressed, and Laurel feeling she had no choice, let the matter drop.

The next morning Lorenzo summoned her to his bedroom, where he was resting. He spent a good part of each day in his bedroom, making Laurel wonder if he had as much time as the doctors had said.

'Are you feeling all right?' Laurel asked, trying not to let anxiety creep into her voice.

'I'm fine.' Lorenzo smiled. 'Just a bit tired, which is nothing unusual in my condition. But I have a favour to ask of you. Quite a large favour, as it happens.'

'Oh?' Laurel came to sit on the edge of his bed,

taking his papery hands between hers. 'If it's within my power, I'll do it.'

'I want to see your mother.' Lorenzo held Laurel's gaze as she tried to hide her surprise. 'I never stopped loving her, and with so little time left, I'd like to spend what there is of it with someone I love.' His questioning smile wavered a little. 'If you think she'll have me?'

'I...' Laurel had no doubt her mother would jump at the chance of finding a secure position, though she hoped Elizabeth would want—and feel—more than that. Was the love still there? Laurel hoped it was for Lorenzo's sake...as well as her mother's. This could be a much-needed reunion and reconciliation for both of them.

'I know you can't really answer that question,' Lorenzo assured her. 'But could you talk to her? Prepare her, a little? And if you could give me her phone number, if you find she would welcome a call...'

'Yes, of course.' What other answer could she give? Yet with a heavy sensation in her stomach Laurel feared how Cristiano would react to her involvement in getting Elizabeth and Lorenzo back together. At best, he'd be coldly contemptuous of such doings. At the worst...completely furious.

Yet looking at Lorenzo's tired, lined face, seeing his wan smile, Laurel knew she couldn't refuse his request. Not for any reason at all.

She called her mother a few minutes later, sitting on a bench in the terraced garden, away from the house and anyone who could listen in.

'Laurel.' Her mother sounded genuinely glad to

hear from her, which was unusual in itself. 'How are you? Where are you? I've been so worried!'

'I'm sorry I haven't been in touch,' Laurel said, although her mother was rarely in touch with her. Still, the apology came of its own accord, as it always had.

'Well, where have you been?'

'With Cristiano.'

Elizabeth drew her breath in sharply. 'Still? He usually tires of women after a week at most.'

Laurel tried to suppress the flash of annoyance and even hurt she felt at her mother's matter-of-fact tone. 'He'll tire of me soon, I suppose.' Sooner even than she'd expected, no doubt, after he found out about this phone call.

'I'm glad to know you're all right.' Elizabeth sniffed. 'I was worried, you know, although I doubt you'll believe me. I never meant things to happen that way with Rico.'

'I know.'

'I thought he just wanted to flirt. I hoped that was all it was, for both of our sakes. I know I've been far from the world's greatest mother, but I don't think I'm that bad.' She let out a wobbly laugh, and then sighed. 'The truth is, I'm too old for him. I'm too old for most men these days. All washed up at forty-six. I'm sorry.'

'I know.' Laurel believed her mother, even if Cristiano would think it was foolish. Her mother never thought out her slap-dash plans, her desperate bids for the life of luxury and security she'd always craved.

'I'm sorry,' Elizabeth said after a moment. 'Truly. But I will need the money from the sale of that house.'

'I know,' Laurel said again. She hadn't deceived

herself that her mother would suddenly have an attack of generosity and give her her half of her grandfather's house free and clear. And she'd decided, after everything, that a house was just a house. She couldn't afford a similar place; in fact, on her salary, she'd barely be able to afford a one-bedroom apartment in town. But after everything it didn't seem to matter quite so much. Home wasn't a farmhouse in Illinois any more. It was wherever Cristiano was, and that was a place she most likely wasn't going to be able to be.

'I'm calling for a reason, though, Mom,' Laurel said, determined to say what she needed to. 'Cristiano and I are staying with Lorenzo.'

Elizabeth drew her breath in again, a quick, audible hiss. 'Oh, yes?' she asked cautiously.

'He'd like to speak to you, on the phone. He asked me to call you first, to see if you'd welcome a call from him.'

Elizabeth didn't speak for a long moment, and when she did her voice was thick with unshed tears. 'Yes,' she said, and cleared her throat. 'Yes, I would very much welcome a call from him.'

Fury boiled through Cristiano's blood like black tar, rising up and choking him. He strode through the villa, glaring into empty rooms in search of the woman who had orchestrated his father's destruction. *How could she?* And without consulting him!

Moments ago he'd left his father's bedroom, stunned past all sensibility. He'd managed to moderate his tone with his father, but Cristiano didn't think he would be able to show such self-control when it came to Laurel.

He found her in the library, a pleasant, book-lined room with views of the side garden, adorned with its orange trees and hibiscus. Laurel was curled up on the sofa, a book lying open next to her, her expression both pensive and wary. She'd been waiting for him, waiting for him to confront her, because she knew what she'd done was wrong.

Cristiano closed the door carefully behind him and stared her down. Laurel lifted her chin, meeting his narrowed gaze with something close to defiance, infuriating him all the more.

'How could you?' he stated quietly, not even a question. 'How *could* you?'

'I assume you're talking about helping your father to be in touch with my mother.'

'She is arriving here tomorrow morning.'

'I know.' Laurel's chin went up another notch. 'I helped to book the flight, a red-eye from New York.'

Cristiano shook his head, trying to keep a rein on his anger. He felt like throttling her. 'My father is in his last months of life, and you want to bring Elizabeth Forrester back into his life?'

'He asked.'

'Of *course* he asked.' Cristiano raked a hand through his close-cropped hair, nails grazing skin, the brief flash of pain an outlet for his frustration. 'He's feeling lonely and vulnerable. He is an eternal optimist when it comes to matters of the heart. And, in every single case, every romantic attachment he's ever made has ended in disaster.'

'What are you afraid of, Cristiano?' Laurel asked quietly. 'Because in this case the disaster is going to happen, no matter what. Your father is going to die.

Why shouldn't we—yes, *we*—help to make his last days and weeks a little bit happier?'

He stared at her in disbelief. 'And you think having Elizabeth here will achieve that aim?'

Something flickered in Laurel's eyes but she kept his gaze. 'I don't know,' she admitted. 'But I hope so.'

'Do I need to remind you that this is the woman who, only two weeks ago, as good as sold you to a very unpleasant man and did nothing while he attacked you?'

'No,' Laurel answered stiffly. 'You don't need to remind me. And it wasn't quite like that—'

'The woman who,' Cristiano continued relentlessly, 'Has been seen with several dozen Z-listers over the last decade? Who is so clearly only with a man for what he can provide for her financially?'

'Is that what you're worried about?' Laurel flung back at him. 'That my mother will take Lorenzo's money? Your inheritance?'

'Hardly.' The single word was scathing. 'I have no need of my father's money, and he obviously won't need it in the long term.' He pressed his lips together. 'No, Laurel, I'm worried about my father's health. His mental and emotional health. How do you think he'll feel if and when Elizabeth abandons him in his greatest moment of need? Don't you think there is a significant chance of her coming here, taking what she can and hightailing it to heaven knows where?'

Laurel pressed her trembling lips together. 'That's a rather cynical view.'

'I have reason to be cynical,' Cristiano snapped. 'Many reasons. I have yet to see a romantic relationship that has actually worked.'

'Not even ours, obviously,' Laurel returned, bitterness spiking every word. 'Not that we have a romantic relationship. Of course I don't dare to presume such a thing.' She rolled her eyes, and Cristiano glared at her, his fists clenched, his chest heaving.

'This isn't about us.'

'Of course it isn't.'

'If you're trying to say something, why don't you just spit it out?'

Laurel took a deep, steadying breath. When she spoke, her voice was quiet, even sad, the bitterness and anger gone. Too bad they were still out in full force in Cristiano. 'The difference between us, Cristiano,' she said slowly, 'Is that I choose to hope and you choose to doubt. And that is a chasm that neither of us seem able to cross.'

'How poetic,' he practically sneered. 'If I'm doubting, it's because I have very good reason to doubt. I've watched your mother swan into one or another of my hotels over the last ten years, always on the arm of some man, always out for herself. That is not the kind of person I want to introduce into my father's life at this point.'

'Too bad you don't have a choice,' Laurel returned evenly. 'He's a grown man, and he can make his own choices. He *asked* me,' she emphasised, her voice throbbing with emotion now. 'He asked me to call her and see if she'd welcome a phone call from him. And she did. There were tears in her voice when she realised he wanted to be in touch.'

'I'm sure there were,' Cristiano dismissed. 'She's a passable actress.'

Laurel shook her head. 'Does it make you happy?'

she asked. 'To feel so bitter and superior all the time? Does it feel good to tear down every possibility of hope and love that you can? Because, if it doesn't, you must be a wretched, unhappy man, and then I would feel very sorry for you.'

Cristiano felt a muscle tick in his clenched jaw. 'The last thing I need,' he ground out, 'is your pity.'

'You have it anyway,' Laurel snapped. Tears shone in her eyes and she blinked them away fiercely. 'Would you really deny your father a chance to be with the woman he loves?'

Yes. Everything in him shouted it. But he stayed silent, because to admit such a thing seemed both callous and cruel. Laurel took a step towards him, one slender hand outstretched.

'What is it you're really afraid of, Cristiano?' she asked softly.

Afraid? He wasn't afraid. Not for himself, anyway. For his father. This wasn't about him, about them, even though Laurel kept trying to make it seem as if it was.

'I'm not afraid. I just don't want to see my father get hurt.'

'If he's willing to take the risk, then you should be as well.'

Cristiano just shook his head. His anger had started to dissipate, replaced by a weary acceptance. He knew Laurel was right; he couldn't keep his father from inviting Elizabeth here, into his life, if he wanted to. He couldn't even keep him from getting hurt. And blaming Laurel for helping a grown man make his own choice was, he knew, unfair.

So all that was left to feel was something close to despair, a deep and unwelcome understanding that

Laurel was right. They *were* different. She held onto hope and he couldn't find it anywhere. He didn't even know how to try.

The last two weeks had been amazing, but they'd been just that. Weeks out of time, apart from reality. What happened if and when it turned out Laurel wasn't pregnant? She'd go back to her life in Illinois and he'd go back to Rome.

He could ask her to stay with him as his mistress, but he knew instinctively that Laurel would reject such a possibility. Perhaps it was better to have a clean break, a swift separation. Perhaps then they could both move on as they needed to.

'Fine,' he said, his voice clipped. 'She can come, and tomorrow you can take that pregnancy test. For both our sakes, I hope it's negative.'

CHAPTER SEVENTEEN

LAUREL STOOD ON the front terrace of Lorenzo's house and watched her mother mount the steps. She'd taken the ferry from Naples, and then the funicular to the centre of Capri, then walked the rest of the way, insisting she didn't need anyone to collect her.

It took Laurel a few moments to realise her mother looked nervous. Her lips, devoid of her usual scarlet lipstick, were pressed together; and, instead of one of her picture-perfect outfits, complete with jewellery, heels, and a face-full of make-up, she wore a simple, loose sundress and sandals. She looked lovely, and every one of her forty-six years.

Laurel started down the steps. 'Mom.' She didn't use the endearment often, but it slipped out now naturally. Elizabeth looked up at her, her face creasing into a smile.

'Laurel.' They embraced, the hug unfamiliar in its rarity, yet still so welcome. The last twelve hours, since her confrontation with Cristiano, had been some of Laurel's worst. After their argument he'd disappeared into the study, and he hadn't come to their bedroom all night. This morning he'd closeted himself again, which Laurel supposed was just as well, as she doubted his presence would add to the happy reunion.

And yet…everything in her ached. Her relationship with Cristiano was as good as over, and she couldn't stand the thought.

'Come on—let me bring you to Lorenzo,' she said, taking her mother's arm.

'How is he?' Elizabeth asked quietly. 'He told me about his illness on the phone. And that…' her voice wavered '…that he doesn't have very long. A few months, maybe.'

'He's perked right up since you told him you were coming. He's missed you.'

'And I've missed him.' Elizabeth shook her head. 'He was the only man I ever really loved, you know. I know I've made a terrible mess of my life in so many ways, but Lorenzo…' Her voice quavered, her eyes bright with tears. 'If only I hadn't squirreled away that stupid money.'

'Don't think about that now—'

'I didn't think of it as stealing. Just…security.' She shook her head. 'If I could go back in time…'

Laurel patted her arm in quiet comfort. 'Let me take you to him.'

She led her mother through the villa to a small sitting room where Lorenzo had been resting and waiting. Now as Laurel opened the door he stood slowly, his face creased in expectation and anxiety.

'Elizabeth.' The single word had a world of meaning, a wealth of memory.

'Lorenzo.'

Laurel didn't need to see or hear any more. The way her mother looked at Lorenzo, and the way he looked at her, was more than enough to assure her she'd done the right thing.

She only wished Cristiano could see it, but then she doubted he would believe even then. He didn't want to believe. She'd come to that realisation during the long, sleepless hours of last night. When it came right down to it, Cristiano was making a choice. He wasn't enslaved to his emotions or lack of them any more than she was. He was making a choice—one he made every day. To live alone. To stay separate. To choose not to love. And somehow, although she couldn't see how now, she was going to have to come to terms with that.

'Laurel.'

Laurel stilled, everything in her tensing with both yearning and alarm as she saw Cristiano standing in the front doorway of the villa. He looked rumpled, sexy and gorgeous in faded jeans that clung to his muscled legs and a T-shirt that lovingly caressed his pecs. His eyes looked silver in his tanned face, a hint of stubble on the clean, hard line of his jaw.

'Yes?' Laurel managed, practically stuttering in her nervousness. She ached for him so much, and she couldn't believe he was simply going to walk away from her. From them.

'I went out and bought this.' He held up a small white paper bag, the kind that came from a pharmacy. Laurel didn't need to ask what the bag held.

She licked her dry lips. 'You want me to take it now?'

Cristiano shrugged. His face was impassive, giving nothing away. 'You might as well.'

Laurel made no move to take the bag. Now that the

moment was here, she didn't want it. Would rather keep not knowing. 'You know, two weeks isn't a magic number,' she said, her voice uneven. 'Some women don't test positive for longer than that.' And there were more sensitive tests that showed a pregnancy at only ten days after conception. Laurel knew that, knew she could have taken a test days ago, but she'd remained silent.

Cristiano arched a dark eyebrow. 'Why don't you take the test and then we'll discuss possibilities?'

With no other option, Laurel took the bag from him and headed upstairs. Cristiano followed.

'I'll wait here,' he said when they were in the bedroom they'd shared since coming to Capri, save for last night. 'It should only take a few minutes.'

Wordlessly Laurel nodded and then barricaded herself in the bathroom. She turned the lock and let out a shuddering breath. The moment of truth.

Fortunately the test came with instructions in English and, squinting to make out the fine print, Laurel read them and then did what was necessary. She turned the test over so she didn't have to look at it and sat on the edge of the bathtub, her heart rollicking within her. Three minutes had never seemed so long.

Outside the bathroom door she could hear Cristiano pacing the bedroom and she wondered what he was thinking. Hoping for. Was there a part of him, like her, who wanted her to be pregnant? Who wanted the choice to be taken away? She knew if she was pregnant Cristiano would marry her as he'd promised. He was a man who'd closed off emotions, yes, but he was also a man of honour.

Laurel tried to imagine what that life would look

like: married to Cristiano, a baby in her arms, then a smiling toddler stumbling on chubby legs while they, the proud parents, looked on. It was a beautiful image, but one that was shrouded in the mists of impossibility. If Cristiano married her simply because of the baby, that code of honour that ran through him like a rod of steel would turn into resentment and bitterness because he'd be living a life he hadn't chosen.

Laurel took a deep breath as she glanced at her watch. Four minutes had passed. There could be no delaying it now. Reaching out slowly, as if it might bite her, she took the pregnancy test and flipped it over. She stared at the single pink line as her heart went into freefall. One line: not pregnant.

Even though she knew in her heart what the test was telling her, she scrambled for the directions and read them again to make sure. One line: not pregnant. It was irrefutable. And, really, she'd known all along. Her cycle was, in this case, depressingly regular.

She threw the test away and washed her hands at the sink, staring hard at her reflection. So she wasn't pregnant. It was better this way. She knew it, felt it, even though part of her still railed against the unfairness of it all. A pregnancy wouldn't have helped anything. In fact, it most likely would have made things worse. So this was a good thing, she told herself as she dried her hands and then tidied her hair, determined to seem composed and even upbeat. In this moment she did not want Cristiano to see how he was crucifying her.

Taking another deep breath, Laurel opened the door. Cristiano stopped his pacing and turned to face her, his expression utterly fathomless. 'Well?' he asked when the silence stretched on for several seconds.

'I'm not.' Laurel spoke flatly, folding her arms across her body, needing to hold herself together.

Cristiano stared at her for a few moments, his gaze assessing, speculative. 'But, as you said before, it is not possible to know for certain at this stage?'

'No, but I'm quite sure, Cristiano, just as I was when you first mentioned the possibility. My period isn't due for another week.'

Something flashed across Cristiano's face too fast for her to discern what it was—disappointment, relief or something else entirely. 'Even so...'

'There's no point, trust me. If by some miracle or twist of chance I was pregnant, I would tell you. But I don't need to stay here until it's irrefutable, for heaven's sake.' *Unless you want me to stay...for my own sake. For ours.*

Neither of them said anything for endless moments, moments where Laurel felt the last, faint, frail thread of hope she'd still nourished fray and then snap. And, because she couldn't bear Cristiano to send her away, she spoke first.

'I suppose I should book my ticket.' She lifted her chin and forced a smile to her lips that felt like a crack in her skin. 'Pack my things. It's...' She swallowed. 'It's been fun, Cristiano.' It had been so much more than that, but what else could she say? Cristiano did fun. He didn't do much more than that. And this entire affair had always been on his terms.

He stared at her for a long moment, his eyes hard, his expression still so unrelentingly inscrutable. 'Yes,' he said finally. 'It has.'

* * *

The next twenty-four hours seemed to go into hyperspeed. From the moment Laurel had walked out of their bedroom to the awful one when she left Capri, Cristiano felt as if everything was moving in a fast blur while he was stuck in slow motion.

His mind felt numb, frozen in the same gear it had been in when Laurel had walked out of the bathroom, her face wiped of expression, her eyes so terrifyingly blank. He used to be able to see everything in her eyes—every thought, every emotion, every hope. But standing there, with the silence yawning between them, he hadn't seen anything.

And then those awful words… *It's been fun.* Such a casual dismissal of everything they'd shared and experienced together. Yet how many times had he said it over the years? The words had tripped off his tongue with thoughtless ease. Sometimes he'd tossed them over his shoulder while strolling out of a room.

And now this.

That evening Cristiano found Laurel in their bedroom, packing a suitcase. Her face was pale and composed; she looked lovely, even peaceful. Perversely Cristiano wanted her to look heartbroken, or at least a little distressed.

She looked up when he entered, her hands stilling on the pile of folded clothes. 'I booked my ticket,' she said, her voice toneless.

Cristiano felt as if everything inside him was coiled so tightly he was going to snap. Fall apart into broken pieces like a clock too tightly wound. 'Have you?' he asked, his tone diffident. Almost.

'Yes; a morning flight from Naples to Rome tomorrow. And then on to Chicago.' She started packing again. 'I'll be home by tomorrow night.'

'Late.'

'Yes.' She resumed packing, her head bent. 'Late.'

Cristiano watched her pack for a few moments and then he realised how little she was actually putting into her one small suitcase. 'Wait,' he said, his voice coming out terse and demanding. 'What are you doing? Why are you not packing all your clothes?'

'I hardly need evening gowns in Canton Heights, Cristiano,' Laurel said without looking up.

An entirely unreasonable indignation rose up in him. 'They're yours. They belong to you. You should take them.'

'They'd require two or even three suitcases,' Laurel returned evenly. 'I don't want to pay the extra baggage allowance for clothes I'm never going to wear.'

'I'll pay it, then,' Cristiano insisted. It suddenly felt important that she take the clothes he'd bought for her, the gifts he'd given.

'And how would I manage to carry all those suitcases?' Laurel asked, a note of exasperation entering her voice. 'I'm taking the funicular to the ferry, and then a bus to the airport and then to the plane. I can't manage it.'

'I'll arrange private transport,' Cristiano said. It seemed simple to him, and for some ridiculous reason he really wanted her to take the clothes with her. 'A car from the villa that will take you all the way to Rome.'

Laurel gazed at him levelly for a moment. 'As eager as you may be to get me out of your life quickly, I'm fine with public transport.'

Cristiano stared at her, silently fuming, because

of course he hadn't meant it that way. But he didn't even know what he had meant, or how to explain. So he stayed silent, and Laurel kept packing, and after a few more tense moments Cristiano turned on his heel and walked out of the room.

He didn't sleep that night, lying awake and gritty-eyed, staring at the ceiling as he went over the last two weeks and kept telling himself this was what he wanted. What he had to want.

Because what was the alternative, really? Their lives were so different. Laurel wasn't going to want to give up her job, or even that house she claimed to love so much. And Cristiano's life was in Italy, managing his hotels and making new business deals. This made sense. This was the only way. It had to be.

He didn't come out of the study when he heard her suitcase bumping down the stairs. Didn't trust himself to say goodbye in the cool, civil way he wanted to. He was being a coward, and he knew it, but the other option—of breaking down or begging her to stay—felt impossible. Unbearable. So he stayed still and listened as the suitcase bumped down each step and then the front door clicked softly shut.

The house suddenly felt deathly silent.

He buried himself in work for the next three days, trying not to think. He didn't sleep, and barely ate. On day four he finally dragged himself up to his father's bedroom, pausing in surprise on the threshold at seeing Elizabeth sitting next to him, smiling at something Lorenzo was saying, her head bent close to his.

The image was arresting in its poignant intimacy. The love was so visible between the two of them, it felt as if it shimmered in the air. Cristiano could hardly credit it, yet he knew it was true. Laurel had been right.

Elizabeth caught sight of him first, her expression freezing before she managed a cautious smile.

'Cristiano,' Lorenzo called, beckoning to him with one gnarled hand. 'Come in.'

'I don't want to disturb…'

'You aren't,' Lorenzo assured him. 'But you look terrible. You miss Laurel.' It was a statement, and one Cristiano chose to ignore.

'You seem well,' he said stiffly, although his father had been spending more and more time resting in bed.

'I feel well.' Lorenzo shot Elizabeth an adoring look. 'I feel very well.'

Cristiano gazed at the two of them, feeling flummoxed, weary, yet strangely cheered. Who was he to deny his father his happiness? Laurel had asked the same question and he'd dismissed it, because he had truly believed Elizabeth Forrester couldn't make his father happy. But, against all odds, it seemed she could.

He left them a short while later, drifting around the house like a ghost. There was no reason to stay here, of course, now that Elizabeth was proving to be such a capable nurse. He could return to Rome, to his penthouse, to his life. All of it felt empty.

'May I talk to you for a few minutes?'

Cristiano turned at the sound of Elizabeth's tense voice. 'Yes,' he answered, as tense as she was.

Elizabeth took a deep breath. 'I know you don't like me, Cristiano. I know you don't trust me. And,' she continued before he could protest against either statement, which he wasn't even sure he would have, 'I know I have not shown myself well in your eyes.' She grimaced. 'I've not shown myself well in my own eyes. I've made a lot of poor choices—choices borne out of fear, but that doesn't excuse them, I know.'

Cristiano felt compelled to say, 'Laurel told me something of your life.'

'Did she? Laurel has always been far more forgiving of me than I deserve. I know that.' She let out an unsteady breath. 'But I want to reassure you, Cristiano, that I love your father. I've always loved him. I know you didn't trust me ten years ago, and you had reason not to—good reason—but the only reason I took that money was because I'd known what it is to be poor and I never wanted to be it again.' She managed a rather wavering smile. 'It was wrong, and I accept that, but I was never going to leave him. I realise there's no reason for you to believe that, though. I don't deserve your trust in that or any matter.'

But Cristiano found he did believe her, much to his chagrin. 'I believe you loved him,' he said. 'And that you love him still. You wouldn't be here otherwise.' He paused. 'But are you really prepared to stay until the end, as difficult as that will be?'

She lifted her chin, reminding him of Laurel. 'Yes, I am, because that's what love does. I didn't come here thinking it would be easy, you know.' Her eyes flashed. 'I've had enough of easy.'

'Have you?' Cristiano asked, more curious than sceptical.

'Yes, I have. Love isn't easy. It's hard and messy and painful, but worth it. I believe that.' Her chin tilted up another notch and her gaze fastened on his, unrelenting in its perception. 'Maybe that's something you need to think about.'

Twenty-four hours later Cristiano stood in front of a small farmhouse of weathered white wood, with a view of rolling fields and a distant glint of the pond Laurel had once told him about. Cristiano let out a long, low breath as he surveyed the house with its bowed front porch and peeling paint that Laurel had thought of as home. Had been willing to risk everything for.

Slowly he mounted the steps; he could tell from the darkened windows and empty driveway that she wasn't home. It was six o'clock in the evening, twilight stealing slowly over the hills, the sound of crickets chirruping in the air.

Cristiano hadn't given a lot of thought to what he would do when he got here. He'd been focused on the how—the travel, the logistics—his mind buzzing and blank with the import of what came next.

And now she wasn't even here.

He peered in the windows, noting the mellow oak floorboards, the hand-made quilt thrown over the back of a squashy sofa, the many photographs on the walls. It was a well-loved home and, for a woman who had been dragged around the globe in search of the next boyfriend and protector, it must have felt like the ultimate sanctuary. No wonder Laurel had wanted to keep it.

But would she want to keep him?

He'd spent his whole life staying emotionally safe. Today he was going to risk it all.

The sound of a car had him turning. A beat-up truck pulled into the drive, and after a few seconds Laurel got out. She was wearing her nurse's scrubs, her hair held back in a ponytail, and she looked tired, lovely and so very, very welcome. Cristiano had to keep himself from catapulting himself off the porch and dragging her into his arms. There were things he had to say first. Things Laurel needed to hear.

She mounted the steps, fishing in her bag for her keys, still not seeing him. Not wanting to startle her, Cristiano said softly, 'Laurel.'

She stilled and then looked up, the blood draining from her face. She swayed slightly where she stood and Cristiano took a step forward.

'Laurel,' he said again, and this time he didn't hide how he felt. It came through in her name, the loveliest word in the world. Laurel's eyes widened and he knew she understood, or at least he hoped she understood.

'Cristiano.' Her voice was a breath. 'What are you doing here?' A wary look came into her eyes. 'I'm not pregnant. For sure.'

'That's not why I came.'

'Why, then?'

'Because I need to tell you that I love you.'

She blinked, looking dazed. 'You…?'

'Love you.' He'd agonised so much about saying it, three little words that cost so much, meant so much, yet suddenly seemed so surprisingly easy to say.

Cristiano felt buoyant and so, so light, as if a huge weight had just tumbled off him. A weight that had never really been there at all, except in the terrible void of his own fears. 'I love you,' he said again, just because he could. 'I was stupid not to realise it before, and even stupider not to say it. Stupid to let you walk away when you're the best thing in my life.' He laughed out loud, amazed at the words tumbling out of him. Amazed at how much he meant them.

'Cristiano…'

For one heart-stopping second he thought she was going to let him down. This was the risk he'd taken, and here was the danger, the awful, awful pay-off. But in the next second he realised it didn't matter. Well, it mattered; of course it mattered. His life was over without Laurel in it. But he would have said it all anyway, no matter what her response, because he needed to. Because he wanted to be a man who admitted his feelings. His love.

'I know I might be too late.' He spoke over her, his voice roughening. 'I know you might have changed your mind, or perhaps you didn't love me in the first place. I wouldn't blame you, considering how I've acted. How afraid I've been. But I'll still say it, because I want you to know. Because you deserve to know, after everything we've had together. After everything I put you through. I was so afraid, Laurel, of what love was. What it meant. How it could make you hurt. I was afraid, and I let that fear control me, but I won't any longer. I refuse to. I love you, Laurel Forrester, and that won't ever change.'

Tears sparkled in her eyes and she let out a trembling laugh. 'Good,' she said, and stepped into his arms. 'Because I love you too, and that won't change either.'

'Thank heaven.' He wrapped his arms around her, breathing her in, savouring the feel of her. 'Because we are done with all this drama, do you hear me? We love each other, we're getting married and we're not spending a single night apart ever again.'

'Back to giving orders, are you?' Laurel asked, tilting her face up to him as her mouth met his in a quick and breath-stealing kiss. 'Good thing I don't mind.'

Cristiano laughed and pulled her closer. 'Good thing,' he agreed in a murmur, and kissed her again.

EPILOGUE

Three Months Later

'YOU LOOK BEAUTIFUL.'

Laurel twitched at her veil as her mother sniffed and dabbed her eyes. 'The most beautiful bride that ever was.'

Laurel managed a tremulous smile. 'As long as Cristiano thinks so,' she said.

'Of course he will,' Elizabeth said. 'The man is mad about you.'

'As Lorenzo is about you.' Laurel met her mother's gaze in the mirror as they shared a sorrowful smile. The last three months had been filled with joy, as well as sadness. Lorenzo was holding his own, and he and Elizabeth were inseparable. But their days together were numbered, and they both knew it, making them all the more determined to seize love and happiness while they could.

While Elizabeth had remained with Lorenzo in Capri, Laurel had stayed for several weeks in Canton Heights to work out her notice, before moving to Rome to be with Cristiano. She'd informed him that she wasn't going to be a good trophy wife any more than she'd been a good mistress—she wanted to work and be active—and Cristiano wholeheartedly agreed. Already she'd joined several committees, including one led by Michel Durand, to help determine public policy on end-of-life care. After ten- and twelve-hour shifts in a hospital, this kind of work was different and invigorating.

But best of all was her life with Cristiano, the easy love they shared. The doubts and fears had fallen away for both of them, leaving nothing but love and joy, shining and pure.

A knock sounded on the door of Laurel's bedroom in Lorenzo's villa, where the wedding was to take place.

'Are you ready?' Ana, the wedding planner, called. 'Everyone is waiting.'

It was going to be a small wedding with a handful of friends from Rome and Capri in the villa's garden, overlooking the sparkling sea. Lorenzo wasn't able to travel and Laurel had never wanted a big ceremony of pomp and circumstance. She took a deep breath, gave her reflection one last, considering glance and turned to the door.

Elizabeth slipped her hand in hers for a quick squeeze before walking out. Laurel had chosen a simple dress as befit the occasion—summery and light, with *broderie anglaise* on the bodice and a gently swinging skirt. A circlet of flowers kept her veil in place and she held a small posy of violets.

Giving her mother a small, nervous smile, she headed downstairs.

The garden was bathed in sunshine, a trio of violins playing soft music as Laurel approached. Guests turned in their seats but she barely noticed, so conscious was she of Cristiano standing under an arbour twined with white roses. He looked magnificent in a navy blue suit, but it was the look on his face that stole Laurel's breath and reminded her that he already had her heart. Pure, shining love, the same as she felt.

The music swelled and, with a smile on her face and a song in her heart, and all the love she felt shining in her eyes, Laurel started down the aisle to meet her groom.

* * * * *

If you enjoyed
THE INNOCENT'S ONE NIGHT SURRENDER
why not explore these other Kate Hewitt stories?

ENGAGED FOR HER ENEMY'S HEIR
THE SECRET HEIR OF ALAZAR
THE FORCED BRIDE OF ALAZAR

Available now!

HARLEQUIN

Presents.

Available January 16, 2018

#3593 THE SECRET VALTINOS BABY
Vows for Billionaires
by Lynne Graham
Merry Armstrong couldn't resist Angel Valtinos's sensual charisma—he awakened her with his touch and left her pregnant! Valtinos's legacy *must* be legitimised, but seducing Merry into marriage will be his biggest challenge...

#3594 A BRIDE AT HIS BIDDING
by Michelle Smart
Undercover journalist Carrie Rivers is playing a dangerous game with Andreas Samaras. When her ruse is revealed, there's only one way to protect Andreas's reputation: blackmail Carrie to the altar!

#3595 CLAIMING HIS NINE-MONTH CONSEQUENCE
One Night With Consequences
by Jennie Lucas
It's not what he wanted, but Ares Kourakis is going to be a father. He'll dutifully marry Ruby, but will intense passion and a vast fortune be enough to get her down the aisle?

#3596 BOUGHT WITH THE ITALIAN'S RING
Conveniently Wed!
by Tara Pammi
Pia Vito is heir to CEO Raphael Mastrantino's billion-dollar empire—so he initiates a calculated seduction! But when inescapable longing engulfs them, to make her his, Raphael must give her more than a diamond ring!

#3597 THE GREEK'S ULTIMATE CONQUEST
by Kim Lawrence

Grief-struck Nik Latsis found oblivion with a stunning stranger. Since then, Chloe's haunted his dreams. Only another taste will rid him of his desire, but first Nik must entice feisty Chloe back into his bed...

#3598 A PROPOSAL TO SECURE HIS VENGEANCE
by Kate Walker

Imogen O'Sullivan is horrified when Raoul breaks up her engagement and makes her his own convenient bride—he's planning a passionate punishment for their stormy past! Can Imogen resist Raoul's delicious revenge?

#3599 REDEMPTION OF A RUTHLESS BILLIONAIRE
by Lucy Ellis

Nik Voronov is ferociously protective of his grandfather. When he believes Sybella Parminter is taking advantage, he strips her of her job! But unexpected desire soon threatens to consume them both...

#3600 SHOCK HEIR FOR THE CROWN PRINCE
Claimed by a King
by Kelly Hunter

Prince Casimir never forgot his wild nights of abandon with Anastasia Douglas. Years later, he discovers she had his daughter! And he'll stop at nothing to claim them both...

Get 2 Free Books,
Plus 2 Free Gifts—
just for trying the
Reader Service!

◆ HARLEQUIN *Presents*®

HP17R3

Ruby.

Pregnant.

Impossible. She couldn't be. They'd used protection.

He could still remember how he'd felt when he'd kissed her. When he'd heard her soft sigh of surrender. How she'd shuddered, crying out with pleasure in his arms. How he'd done the same.

And she'd been a virgin. He'd never been anyone's first lover. Ares had lost his virginity at eighteen, a relatively late age compared to his friends, but growing up as he had, he'd idealistically wanted to wait for love. And he had, until he'd fallen for a sexy French girl the summer after boarding school. It wasn't until summer ended that his father had gleefully revealed that Melice had actually been a prostitute, bought and paid for all the time. *I did it for your own good, boy. All that weak-minded yearning over love was getting on my nerves. Now you know what all women are after—money. You're welcome.*

Ares's bodyguard closed the car door behind him with a bang, causing him to jump.

"Sir? Are you there?"

Turning his attention back to his assistant on the phone, Ares said grimly, "Give me her phone number."

Two minutes later, as his driver pulled the sedan smoothly down the street, merging into Paris's evening traffic, Ares listened to the phone ring and ring. Why didn't Ruby answer?

When he'd left Star Valley, he'd thought he could forget her.

Instead, he'd endured four and a half months of painful celibacy, since his traitorous body didn't want any other woman. He couldn't forget the soft curves of Ruby's body, her sweet mouth like sin. She hadn't wanted his money. She'd been insulted by his offer. She'd told him never to call her again.

And now…

She was pregnant. With his baby.

He sat up straight as the phone was finally answered.

"Hello?"

Don't miss
CLAIMING HIS NINE-MONTH CONSEQUENCE,
available February 2018 wherever
Harlequin Presents® books and ebooks are sold.

www.Harlequin.com

HARLEQUIN
Presents®

Next month, look out for Kelly Hunter's Harlequin Presents debut! Her sinful Claimed by a King quartet stars four powerful rulers, dedicated to duty—until they meet the only women to threaten their iron resolve! In *Shock Heir for the Crown Prince*, Anastasia kept their child a secret. Now Casimir will make her his royal queen…

Prince Casimir of Byzenmaach can't shake the memory of Anastasia Douglas. With her, he forgot his royal duties in a moment of wild abandon. Seven years later, he must wed—but in seeking out the unforgettable Anastasia, he discovers a secret: she gave birth to his daughter! And he'll stop at nothing to claim them both…

Shock Heir for the Crown Prince
Available February 2018!

King Theodosius must find a queen—so he offers Princess Moriana an initiation in the pleasures of the marriage bed…

Convenient Bride for the King
Available March 2018!

And look for Augustus of Arun's and Valentine of Thallasia's stories
Coming soon!

HPBPA0118

Want to give in to temptation with steamy tales of irresistible desire?

Check out **Harlequin® Presents®**, **Harlequin® Desire** and **Harlequin® Kimani™ Romance** books!

New books available every month!

CONNECT WITH US AT:

Harlequin.com/Community

 Facebook.com/HarlequinBooks

Twitter.com/HarlequinBooks

Instagram.com/HarlequinBooks

Pinterest.com/HarlequinBooks

ReaderService.com

ROMANCE WHEN
YOU NEED IT

PGENRE2017